Shop till you drop!

"Oooh," Ellen sighed dreamily as we walked into the jewelry store. "Did you see those to-die-for unicorn pendants in the window?"

"Are they expensive?" I asked.

Ellen looked closely. "I can't find a price. But they're platinum."

I waved my hand dismissively. "Let's buy them," I told Ellen. "There are, what, five of us in the club? Let's get one for everybody."

Ellen's mouth opened as wide as a saucer. "Lila!"

"You don't know how much these cost," Jessica said, staring at the display. "I bet they're not exactly cheap. In fact—"

I held up my hand to interrupt her and turned to Ellen. "Get them, would you?"

Nodding, Ellen scurried away and soon found a salesclerk to help her.

I flagged down the other clerk in the store. "Give me five of these necklaces, please," I demanded, pointing to a case filled with diamonds and pearls.

The clerk's jaw dropped. "Five?" she repeated.

"Five," I said testily. "Do I have to take my business someplace else?" I dropped the gold card on the counter.

Bantam Books in THE UNICORN CLUB series.
Ask your bookseller for the books you have missed.

THE UNICORN CLUB®

LILA ON THE LOOSE

Written by
Alice Nicole Johansson

Created by
FRANCINE PASCAL

BANTAM BOOKS
NEW YORK · TORONTO · LONDON · SYDNEY · AUCKLAND

To Benson Baker Bobrick

RL 4, 008-012

LILA ON THE LOOSE
A Bantam Book / November 1996

Sweet Valley High® *and The Unicorn Club*®
are registered trademarks of Francine Pascal.

Conceived by Francine Pascal.

Produced by Daniel Weiss Associates, Inc.
33 West 17th Street
New York, NY 10011.

Cover art by James Mathewuse.

ISBN: 0-553-48400-1
Published simultaneously in the United States and Canada

Bantam Books are published by Bantam Books, a division of Bantam
Doubleday Dell Publishing Group, Inc. Its trademark, consisting of the
words "Bantam Books" and the portrayal of a rooster, is Registered in U.S.
Patent and Trademark Office and in other countries. Marca Registrada.
Bantam Books, 1540 Broadway, New York, New York 10036.

PRINTED IN THE UNITED STATES OF AMERICA

OPM   0 9 8 7 6 5 4 3 2 1

One

"I am so incredibly excited," I told Jessica Wakefield as I leaned forward in the hair stylist's chair. "I can't believe this is happening to me!"

"Better believe it, Lila," Jessica said. "But if you don't hold still, you better believe you'll lose your ear!"

Oops! I could feel the scissors coming a little too close for comfort. I forced my neck muscles to stay where they were.

"Thank you, Miss Fowler," the stylist said. According to the tag she wore, her name was Gina. "What high school do you go to?"

It was Sunday afternoon. And it was going to be one of the best days of my entire life.

You might think that sounds a little strange coming from me, Lila Fowler. After all, most of the time I hate Sunday afternoons. They mean the end of the weekend is near—and so is the end of free-dom. Who wants to stop a perfectly fun weekend to start school? I mean, give me a break.

But this Sunday was different. Believe it or not, I'd gotten an A on my math test the week before. That's right—an A. As in *awesome!* Mrs. Larson had written *Wow!* and *Good work, Lila!* on my paper and circled the grade with red ink. I wouldn't say it's the first A I've ever gotten, but the last ones were kind of ancient history, if you get my drift.

Naturally I had to tell all my friends. Especially the other members of the Unicorn Club. That's Mandy Miller, Ellen Riteman, Kimberly Haver, and Jessica. Plus me, of course. The Unicorns are the greatest club in Sweet Valley Middle School, where I'm in seventh grade. (Not high school. Yet!) Oh, Ellen did ask what the big deal was, and Mandy had gotten an A too. Still, they were pretty supportive. And isn't that what friends are for?

But the most supportive person was my dad. I'm sure you've heard of my dad, George Fowler of Fowler Enterprises. Not to brag or anything, but he's probably the richest man in Sweet Valley, maybe even in all of southern California. He owns about half the businesses in town, so he's a very busy man. He loves me a lot, of course—I'm his only daughter, after all—but sometimes he doesn't get to spend all the time he wants with me. If your father is rich too, I'm sure you know what I'm talking about.

Anyway, Dad was just as thrilled about my A as I

was. Maybe even more. He'd clapped me on the back and said he was "tremendously proud" of me. Yup, those were his exact words. "Tremendously proud." And—the best part—he said he'd take me out to Chez François for dinner Sunday night to celebrate.

That's right, Sunday.

Like, that night!

Which is why I was at the mall with Jessica, getting my hair done so I'd look my best for Chez François.

"She's not in high school," Jessica told Gina, the stylist. "She's in seventh grade, like me."

I shot Jessica a withering glance. "Who asked you?" I said.

"Only seventh grade?" Gina asked. She swung me around so I could see the back of my head in the mirror. "Well, you certainly could have fooled me."

I decided Gina would get a really big tip. I stuck out my tongue at Jessica. "I just can't believe it," I said again. "Me, getting an A on a math test!"

"You said that already," Jessica said. "Like, maybe twelve times."

I ignored her. "You know that last problem, where we had to reduce the fraction?" I asked. "Well, I just kept reducing and reducing, and I thought I was done. I was just going to turn in the test—and then I heard this little voice in my head!"

I really did, you know. It was so weird the way it happened. I've always thought I'm kind of psychic. Maybe that little voice just proves it.

"Let me guess," Jessica said. "It told you the

fraction could be reduced even more."

"That's right!" I looked at Jessica in surprise, wondering how she knew. "And then I realized that three sixths is the same as one half, duh, and I wrote that in, and—"

"And you got an A," Jessica finished for me. She yawned.

Well, so much for you, Jessica Wakefield, I thought. But I was too happy to be really mad. "I aced it," I said aloud, and I gave her a thumbs-up. "And now Dad is taking me out to dinner!"

"Hold still, please, Miss Fowler," Gina said.

Miss Fowler. I smiled. I liked being called that. Most of the stylists at the salon call me "dear." Or "honey." As if I were just a kid or something.

Maybe I would leave Gina a *gigantic* tip.

"Jessica?" I asked. "I was wondering if you wanted the latest facial treatment. I'll pay." Why not? I was feeling generous. And Jessica is probably my very best friend. Even though she drives me crazy sometimes.

"Oh, you'll like that," Gina said to her. "It's Mississippi mud packs wrapped around steel wool."

Jessica shuddered. "No thanks, Lila," she said.

I shrugged. Which was the wrong thing to do. Gina's scissors came awfully close to my ear again.

I sat as still as I could and let my mind wander. Once in a while I get a little jealous of my friends. They all have fathers who can spend more time with them than mine can. Kimberly, Jessica, and

Mandy all have fathers who are busy, but they're not busy like my dad. Ellen's parents are divorced, but her dad still spends most weekends with her.

On the other hand, my dad needs to go out and earn enough money so that I can have the latest skin treatments and all these trips to the beauty salon. I'd bought myself this incredibly amazing outfit for our dinner that night, and let's face it, the whole thing cost a lot more money than my friends can afford. I'm not saying that to brag or anything; that's just the way it is. Dad works hard, and that helps make my dreams come true.

So you see, it's not totally bad that he has such a horrendous schedule. In a lot of ways, he does it all for me.

I also knew that this dinner would be extra special. Some parents don't want to have anything to do with their kids until they're, you know, intellectually mature. I saw that on a TV talk show last week. Now, I'm old for my age in a lot of ways; anybody will tell you that. But my A in math just proves that I'm intellectually mature too. You probably know exactly what I'm talking about!

When I think of the way Dad and I used to spend time together, I have to laugh. I was such a *kid* back then! There was this dorky dance we used to do together. It was called the Salty Dog Rag or something. I never did figure out how a dog could be salty. Anyway, he'd put on the tape, and we'd dance around the ballroom for what seemed like hours. I didn't exactly know the steps. But then, neither did he.

They sang on the tape too. The first line went "Oh, away down yonder in the state of Arkansas." Talk about old-fogeyville! But you know, the strange thing is, it was actually kind of fun, in a weird way. I can still remember how he'd wrap up my little hand in his big one.

But that's not the way to deal with your daughter when she's thirteen and just got an A on a math test.

On a *hard* math test.

I could just see us that night at Chez François. I'd be wearing my new dress, and I'd behave like the real young lady I've become, not the silly little kid I—ahem—*used* to be. We'd have an adult kind of conversation, and maybe Dad would buy a small perfume company for us to run together.

And things would just go on getting better and better. I smiled to myself. It would be the start of something new.

"There!" Gina said. She turned a small hand mirror this way and that and showed me my new style.

"It looks totally awesome," I said, nodding slowly. And it did. I felt about three years older, and I looked it too.

"It's nice," Jessica admitted.

"Anything else we can do for you today, ma'am?" Gina asked.

Ma'am. I settled back into the chair.

An absolutely superhumongous tip sounded about perfect, I decided.

*   *   *

"The one that really gave me fits was the third problem," I told Jessica. We were making our way to the mall entrance, and I was still thinking about the math test. "Remember the one where you had to—"

But Jessica wasn't listening. "Let's stop at Casey's," she suggested.

"Casey's?" I frowned. "You're kidding, right?"

I like going to Casey's ice-cream parlor as much as anybody. In fact, it's one of the unofficial meeting places for the Unicorn Club. Their peanut-brittle fudge frozen yogurt is absolutely out of this world. But it didn't make sense to go there two hours before meeting my dad at Chez François!

"Of course I'm not kidding," Jessica said. "I don't know about you, but I'm starved."

I shook my head. "Let's not," I protested. But my mouth was watering. Casey's mocha chip crunch was pretty good too. "We'll ruin our appetites."

"Who cares?" Jessica asked. "I don't think you have to worry about ruining your appetite for duck *à l'orange* or pheasant under glass or whatever you're planning to eat tonight."

"Well—" I began.

"But you *can* ruin your appetite for meat loaf," Jessica went on. "And I for one intend to."

I shook my head. Of all the Unicorns, Jessica's the one who's hardest to argue with. When she gets an idea into her head, it stays there! And if I ordered only a single scoop, with no whipped cream—well, I couldn't spoil my appetite much, right?

We found a booth and ordered. At the last minute I decided to get a low-fat vanilla shake. It seemed like a more *mature* thing to get. Jessica ordered a double fudge sundae with extra nuts.

Figures.

"You know what?" I asked. "I didn't even study really hard for that test! That's the most amazing thing. I mean, I studied, sure, but I just didn't study really *hard*. I thought I would get a C or maybe a B, but—"

Jessica interrupted. "You know, I don't see what the big deal is," she said, playing with her fork.

"What the big deal is?" I stared at my friend. "What are you talking about?"

Jessica shrugged. "Oh, everything," she said. "Getting an A. And eating with your dad. I eat dinner with my dad just about every night, and I don't get my hair done for the occasion."

"Oh." I stuck out my bottom lip. Jessica probably didn't know it, but her comment kind of bothered me. "I guess most people wouldn't make a big deal out of it," I said. "But remember, I *don't* eat dinner with my dad very often. He's just too busy. So it's very special for us to have some private time together." I smiled. "And from now on, things will be different," I predicted.

"Whatever." Jessica shrugged. "I just don't get it."

Jessica wouldn't, I thought with a sudden flash of understanding. Her dad's a lawyer, so he doesn't have to work as hard as my dad does. Plus she's got a twin sister, Elizabeth, and an older brother, Steven. So she always has a family member to eat dinner with.

Also, she has a mom. I don't really have a mom, and sometimes I get a little sensitive about not having one. Oh, I *have* one, all right, if you know what I mean. But she isn't exactly there for me the way Mrs. Wakefield is there for Jessica. She lives somewhere in Europe now, and I haven't seen her since I was a baby.

So Dad's all I've got. Unless you count Richard, the chauffeur, and Mrs. Pervis, who keeps house for Dad and me. But they're paid staff. It isn't the same thing.

I sloshed ice cubes around in the bottom of my water glass. "Dad's pretty special to me," I said slowly. "And I'm pretty special to him too. No offense or anything," I added quickly, suddenly realizing that Jessica might take that the wrong way. "I mean, I know you're pretty special to your own dad and all, but—"

I paused. *But it isn't quite the same,* I thought.

Jessica shrugged again. "OK," she said. "I just think it's kind of strange to get your hair done just so you can have dinner with your dad."

I reminded myself that Jessica had probably never been to Chez François for a private dinner with her father.

And I reminded myself that this was going to be the start of some real quality time for my own dad and me.

My eyes met Jessica's. I smiled.

"It's one of the biggest nights of my life," I said. "And everything is going to be one hundred percent perfect."

Two

"There is nothing better than a double fudge sundae from Casey's," Jessica said lazily. She dipped her spoon into her bowl and scooped up some fudge. "Absolutely nothing."

I nodded, watching her eat. My mouth watered. Ordering the low-fat vanilla shake had seemed like a good idea at the time. But it would have been a better idea if mine had come with whipped cream too.

And hot fudge mixed in.

And extra nuts, and a maraschino cherry on top.

Or if Jessica had ordered the same thing I did instead of that incredibly delicious-looking sundae.

I swallowed hard. "It does look good," I said.

"It is," Jessica agreed. She swirled her tongue around the spoon, licking off whipped cream. "This is, like, the ultimate in late-afternoon snacks."

I couldn't take my eyes off the sundae. "It *really* looks good," I said, hoping that Jessica would take the hint and offer me a bite.

Or maybe two or three.

I concentrated on sending thought waves to Jessica. *Share—share—share.* I made the word echo through my mind. Just in case, I leaned a little closer. *Give me a bite—give me a bite—*

"Hey, Lila!" Jessica looked up suddenly.

"Oh, well, if you insist," I said automatically. But then I realized that Jessica wasn't exactly looking at me. She was staring at something over my left shoulder.

"What do you know?" Jessica whispered. Her eyes lit up. "Isn't that Jimmy Lancer sitting over there?"

"Jimmy Lancer?" I spun around as quickly as I could. And my heart started beating a mile a minute.

I guess I should explain about Jimmy Lancer. Jimmy goes to Sweet Valley High School, where he plays on the soccer team. He plays center halfback or left wing or right goalie or something like that, and he's really good. He's incredibly cute too. He has perfect teeth, a great smile, and the most gorgeous curly dark hair this side of Hollywood. To tell you the truth, I think he could be a movie star if he really wanted to.

So what did he have to do with me? Well, a few weeks earlier I'd told the other Unicorns that Jimmy and I had gone on a date. I said that he'd asked me out and we'd hit it off pretty well and he liked me and I liked him and we'd be going out together. I thought they'd be impressed. I mean, after all, Jimmy's in *high school*. But they didn't believe me. Kimberly even accused me of making it up to get everybody's attention.

Actually, Jessica came to my defense. She said I didn't have enough imagination to tell a story like that. I wasn't sure if I should have been pleased or insulted. Especially because—well, you see, the thing is, I *did* kind of make it up. The truth is, I met him. Once. And I introduced myself. And he said hi.

And that was about it. Some hot romance, huh?

That's why Jimmy Lancer was kind of a touchy subject for me.

"Oh, Jimmy," I said, smiling as broadly as I could. "Sure, that's Jimmy. I'd know him anywhere."

Jimmy had his back toward us and was sitting with a bunch of other guys from the soccer team. They were all in their sweats, and their Sweet Valley High soccer gym bags were hanging from the backs of their chairs. Their hair was wet and neatly combed. As I watched, Jimmy leaned forward and pointed at one of the other guys. Everybody laughed.

"He seems to be pretty popular," Jessica observed.

I nodded. "Oh, he's popular, all right," I said, forcing a grin. "Now, Jessica, about that sundae—"

But Jessica wasn't listening. "Aren't you going to go say hello to him?" she asked.

I'd been hoping she wouldn't say that. I mean, what was I going to say? *Hi, Jimmy! I'm sure you've totally forgotten me, but I've told all my friends that we're madly in love. And, by the way, my name's Lila.*

Yeah, right.

I got my thoughts together. No matter what my friends may say about me, I do have them. Thoughts, I mean. "Oh, no," I said, and I gave a little giggle. "He's, um, with his buddies now. I wouldn't dream of interrupting him after practice."

Jessica frowned. "Don't be such a dork," she said severely. "Go say hi. And while you're at it, you can introduce me. Maybe Jimmy's got a brother who's our age but goes to private school or something."

I giggled again, hoping that Jessica didn't expect me to say anything. I was completely clueless about whether Jimmy had a brother at all, let alone one who was our age. In fact, I was completely clueless about Jimmy Lancer in general. I took another sip of my shake. Then I pushed it away, deciding that low-fat vanilla shakes tasted like tofu.

Especially when your so-called best friend has ordered a double fudge sundae just to torment you.

"Aw, c'mon," Jessica said. She twirled her spoon. "Only a loser wouldn't go say hi to a guy she's gone out with."

I felt my cheeks turning red. They do that a lot. Someday someone will invent an antiblusher. You'll be able to spray it on your cheeks any time you think you're about to blush, and you won't. Whoever invents it will make a zillion dollars. "We have this, um, understanding," I said, desperately searching for an excuse. "See, when we're together, we're, like, together. But when we're on our own, well—" I struggled for a way to say it. "Well, we're on our own!"

Jessica groaned. "What kind of a relationship is *that*?" she demanded. "Who came up with such a bogus idea anyway—you or him?" She popped another spoonful into her mouth. Hot fudge trickled down her chin, but I decided not to tell her about it.

"Well," I said, stalling for time, "it was kind of, you know, a joint decision."

Which was true, when you thought about it.

Jessica pushed back her chair. "Look, Lila," she said with her mouth full, "this is crazy. I'll go talk to him myself if you're too shy." She started to stand up.

Uh-oh. "Too shy?" I said, pretending to be shocked. I put my hand on my chest and let my jaw drop open. "Don't be silly, Jessica," I said in as calm a voice as I could manage.

Do I have a choice? I wondered as I pushed my own chair back and stood up myself.

Of course I didn't. No way was I about to let Jessica anywhere near my boyfriend!

Especially since he wasn't actually my boyfriend at all.

I walked to Jimmy's table as slowly as possible.

Maybe I could pretend I'd said hi. Maybe Jessica would get up and go to the bathroom or something. Then I could slide back into my seat and tell her we'd had this really terrific conversation and—

I glanced back at Jessica out of the corner of my eye. No good. She was watching me like a hawk.

I took a deep breath and stepped forward again, wishing I'd never heard of Jimmy Lancer. I was only about three feet away from Jimmy by this time. I could almost reach out and touch him, but the guys still hadn't noticed me.

"Could you believe what Wheatley did on that penalty kick today, man?" Jimmy was saying. "When de Silva cut loose with that shot, I said to myself, 'There's no way he's gonna miss.'"

"Wheatley was, like, ten feet out of position," another one of the boys said. He was tall and blond, and there was a sneer on his face.

Jimmy shook his head. "Was not either, Newcombe. See, de Silva likes to kick with his left foot."

"He does?" A kid with a crew cut looked surprised. "Gee, I've been playing with him for two years now, and I never noticed."

"Well, you gotta start noticing these things," Jimmy said cheerfully. He picked up his water glass. "So anyway, de Silva always kicks lefty, but this time he crossed everybody up and—"

I decided I'd waited long enough. I gave a little cough.

"—the ball sails off to the right, boom!" Jimmy went on, completely ignoring me. He thrust his glass out to show where the ball had gone. "Certain goal, right? But Wheatley dives and gets a hand on it! Greatest play of the century."

I coughed again, louder this time. But Jimmy didn't look up. He took a sip of his water. "Of the century!" he repeated.

At that rate it would be the next century before Jimmy heard me. Coughing wouldn't do it, that was clear. I put on my best smile and fluttered my eyelashes. Mandy Miller says fluttering my eyelashes makes me look especially attractive. Then I lurched toward the table before I could change my mind.

"Oh, Jimmy!" I squealed, pretending I just happened to be walking by. "Wow, what a surprise!"

"Um—hi," Jimmy said, turning around. For the briefest of seconds his eyes looked blank, but then I thought I saw a flash of recognition. Hey, if he remembered my name, I'd be happy.

I put my hand up to pat my hair, hoping he'd notice my nice new *expensive* cut. "It's so cool to run into you like this!" I said in my sweetest voice.

"Yeah," Jimmy said. He smiled. It was an even more gorgeous grin than I'd remembered. "So, um, what brings you here?"

"Oh, you know," I said with a shrug. "The ice cream, mostly." I giggled. "Is practice over?" I asked, trying to make a little more conversation.

"Duh, hey," the blond kid said, staring at me. "Why do you think our hair's all wet, huh?"

"Must be raining," Crew Cut said in a silly voice. He stuck his hand out from under an imaginary umbrella. "Gee, they better fix the roof!"

OK, so it was a pretty stupid comment. I couldn't help turning red.

Now I *really* wished I had some antiblushing spray.

Jimmy waved his hand at his teammates. "Ah, cut it out, guys," he told them.

Jimmy Lancer was coming to my rescue! I drew in my breath and smiled down at him, the way I'd seen a glamorous starlet do to a cute guy in some old black-and-white movie I'd seen on cable a couple of weeks earlier. "Thanks, Jimmy," I murmured.

Jimmy looked a little embarrassed. "No problem," he assured me. And for the first time, our eyes met.

Zing! My heart gave a leap. I'd never really seen Jimmy's eyes so close up before. I couldn't believe how incredibly beautiful they were. Just exactly the right shade of brown.

I leaned forward a little, the way the movie star had, hoping the moment would never end, hoping that Jimmy would just keep staring into my eyes for the rest of his life. I could feel a rush of excitement, a spark. I held my breath. There was something there. Something between Jimmy and me.

Like in that movie. There had been this electricity between the man and the woman when she'd looked at him like that and he'd looked back at her. And it had been real. They hadn't been just acting, I could tell. It was an incredibly romantic moment.

Just like this one!

Jimmy's eyes seemed to pull me in. My hand groped along the tabletop for support. Any moment, I thought, he'd take me in his arms and kiss me. There was this electricity in the air. It was as if we were the only two people in the entire world.

I opened and shut my fingers, trying to find the edge of the table. Our eyes were still locked. He had the most expressive, understanding eyes in the world. You could tell that he was a totally caring, sensitive guy. Not a wimp or anything, of course. Strong and rugged too. And passionate. But mostly—

All of a sudden I realized that my hand was clammy.

And in the next instant I heard raucous laughter coming from the kids around the table.

Suddenly the world wasn't just Jimmy and me anymore. I jerked my hand back. It was dripping with whipped cream and chunks of banana.

I couldn't believe it! I'd put my hand in Jimmy's banana split!

"Put her on that home video show!" Crew Cut was shouting. "Hey, Newcombe, where's your camcorder?"

I stared in horror at the mushy mess all over my

hand. *Ugh, gross!* One moment Jimmy and I were actually clicking—and the next I was some dumb little kid who couldn't even keep her fingers out of an ice-cream bowl! I blinked back tears.

"Hey, she said it was really *cool* to run into him," another boy chimed in. "*Cool* is right!"

"Perfect aim!" Newcombe jeered. "Hey, Lancer, you put that ice cream there on purpose?"

Crew Cut pretended to speak into a microphone. "In other news today, some ditzy middle-school kid put her hand in Jimmy Lancer's banana split. It just goes to show you that Jimmy's fans will do *anything* to get a souvenir of their favorite soccer player." He snickered. "Now back to your regularly scheduled program."

There were no extra napkins on the table. I was ready to run into the ladies' room for paper towels—and maybe a good cry—when I felt pressure against my hand. I looked down. Jimmy was wiping me clean with his own napkin! "Cut it out, you losers," Jimmy told his friends. "Can't you see she's upset?"

"I—I didn't do it on purpose," I stammered, feeling my cheeks about to turn red again. His fingers brushed my palm. It felt wonderful. "I just—I didn't—"

"I know." Jimmy turned to his buddies. "Hey, it happens to everyone. Remember when you fell into the Gatorade at practice last week, Newcombe?"

The blond kid gestured angrily with his spoon.

"That was different!" he protested.

"Into the *Gatorade?*" A kid with shaggy hair stared at Newcombe, a smile playing around his mouth. "I knew you were a klutz, but how'd you manage *that?*"

I breathed a sigh of relief. The soccer players were looking at Newcombe now. They'd forgotten me. I shut my eyes and concentrated on the pressure of Jimmy's hand against mine. Firm but gentle. Like his voice. And his eyes . . .

I shivered. I'd take the whole package. No question about it, Jimmy Lancer was to die for.

The table was suddenly quiet. I snapped my eyes open. Jimmy was smiling at me, his hand still resting on my palm.

"Hey, guys," he said. "Like you to meet a friend of mine. Lila, um—" He frowned.

"Fowler," I tried to say. But my lips wouldn't move. My heart was pounding so hard I thought it would jump out of my chest. *A friend of mine,* he'd called me. Those were his exact words!

"Well, whatever." Jimmy grinned, showing his perfectly even teeth. "Lila, the prettiest girl at Sweet Valley Middle School." He paused. "I guess that'll do for a last name."

If Jimmy hadn't been practically holding my hand the way he was, I would have fallen over dead on the spot.

"Yeah, right," Newcombe began to jeer, but Jimmy just glanced at him, and he shut up.

I blushed. That time I'm positive I got redder than a fire engine.

Jimmy smiled once more and pulled his hand away. "Well, see you around, Lila," he said with a wink.

I knew I was being given the brush-off, but I didn't even care. I darted back to my table, and I don't think my feet ever touched the ground. It's amazing that I didn't bump into anything, because all I could see was Jimmy Lancer's face bobbing in front of me.

Jimmy Lancer's face. I had the feeling I'd be seeing a lot of it in the days and weeks to come.

"Aren't you glad you said hi?" Jessica asked sarcastically. But I barely even heard her.

It looked like there really *was* a connection between me and Jimmy.

And, like a fool, I'd never even noticed!

Three

Chez François is a pretty special place. It's got dim little lights and tiny tables with candles on them. You get about six forks, and the meals are served by these great-looking guys in tuxes who sort of glide from table to table murmuring things in French. They never write down your order either. They just memorize it.

The walls are cool too. There are pictures of François—that's the head chef, who owns the place— shaking hands with practically everybody. Presidents, if you like that kind of thing, and a few movie stars, which is a little more my style. No pictures of Johnny Buck, though. I guess the Buckster doesn't care for crisped shrimp in mustard fruit sauce.

And come to think of it, it's kind of hard to imagine him shaking hands with François.

Up in one corner there's a shot of François shaking hands with my dad. I couldn't see it from where I was sitting, but I knew Dad was up there.

The problem was, he wasn't down here.

I looked at my watch for the gazillionth time. "He's forty-five minutes late now!" I grumbled to myself. I looked around the dining room, hoping I'd catch Dad striding in, out of breath, ready to apologize profusely for being so incredibly late.

But all I could see were couples huddled around the tables, and a waiter sailing across the room, a tray balanced on the tips of his fingers.

Dad, where are you? I wanted to shout.

I'd spent hours getting everything just right—my hair, my dress, my lipstick (the shade was called Pale Amaryllis; it went great with my pearl necklace). Richard and I had even left a few minutes early in case the Sunday evening traffic was bad.

François himself had come out of the kitchen to greet me. He'd told the maître d' (that's, like, the headwaiter) to give me the best table. Then I'd ordered sparkling cider and a couple of appetizers, and I'd relaxed, expecting Dad to show up at any moment. . . .

And I'd been sitting alone at a table for two. For almost an hour.

I didn't know whether to be worried, angry, or sad.

Dad hadn't called the restaurant, that was for sure. I'd asked the maître d' twenty minutes earlier if there were any messages from him. At least, if

Dad *had* called the restaurant, they weren't telling me. I checked my watch again. *If you don't show up in three minutes, Dad,* I threatened him in my mind, *you're dead meat.*

Everyone in the room was staring at me. I could feel it. I could practically hear them snickering across the candles and white tablecloths. I was positive they were asking, *Who's that loser all by herself?* I scrunched down behind my menu, sipping nervously from my third glass of sparkling cider.

I wished Jimmy Lancer were with me. *We could have a really deep conversation while we waited,* I thought. *He'd smile across the table at me and lift his glass of sparkling cider in a suave kind of way and his eyes would twinkle. . . .*

JIMMY: Well, Lila, cheers. (We would clink glasses.) Here's to the most beautiful girl in Sweet Valley Middle School.

ME (blushing, but only enough so that Jimmy would think my cheeks were really rosy): Thanks, Jimmy. Here's to the handsomest guy at Sweet Valley High.

JIMMY (chuckling): It's so sweet of you to say so, Lila. You know, your cheeks seem extra rosy tonight.

ME (going for broke): It's only because I'm with you, Jimmy. . . .

I turned around quickly at the sound of a man's voice. But it was only one of the other customers. Not Dad.

Where are *you, Dad?*

I bit my lip, careful not to chew away all the Pale

Amaryllis. *Maybe he's just, you know, a little delayed,* a voice inside my head told me. *Maybe he got stuck in traffic. Hey, it happens. Just because he's late doesn't mean he's forgotten about me.*

But there was a tight feeling in the pit of my stomach.

What if he *had* forgotten?

I considered using the pay phone to call home. Or maybe I could get his cell phone. But the thought of getting up in front of all those people was nauseating. They'd think I was being stood up.

Scratch that. They'd *know* I was.

Quickly I glanced at my watch. Four minutes had gone by since the last time I'd checked. I sighed. Maybe I'd give him a little more time. Just in case.

"All right, Dad," I said to myself. "If you don't show up in the next two minutes, I'll know you don't really care about me—"

I gasped. A waiter had slunk up so quietly I hadn't even noticed. *"Mademoiselle?"* he purred.

"You scared me!" I said.

The waiter bowed slightly. "I apologize," he said in a deep, rich, French-accented voice. He held out one arm toward my menu. "Pair-haps I may take your or-dair?"

I felt my pulse return to normal. "No, I'm not ready to or-dair—I mean, *order*."

The waiter stood perfectly straight and inclined his head about half an inch. "Very good, *mademoiselle*."

"I'm expecting someone," I went on, gesturing

at Dad's place. "He'll be here any minute now."

"Ah." The waiter's dark eyes gleamed. Was it my imagination, or was that a little smirk at the corners of his lips? "Of course, *mademoiselle*. You are expecting someone."

"That's what I said," I snapped. Suddenly everything about the waiter bugged me. His hair was too perfect. His bow tie was too straight. He looked like a movie star. Like an athlete, not a waiter. Like a soccer player or—

A soccer player. I thought of the way Jimmy's hand had felt on my palm and the way his eyes had melted into mine earlier that day. My heart jumped.

"Very good, *mademoiselle*." The waiter bowed low, and I tumbled back to reality. That smirk was still on his face.

"I'll have you fired if you bother me again," I threatened him. "Don't come back until my dad's here." I narrowed my eyes and stared at him. Jessica calls it my wicked-stepmother imitation, and I do it pretty well, if I do say so myself.

"*Oui, mademoiselle*," he said softly. The next thing I knew, he was gone.

I wondered which of my forks it would be most polite to stab him with if he came back.

That silly French accent bugged me most of all, I decided as I looked at the menu. I told myself that he probably wasn't even French. He'd probably gone to Sweet Valley High, and the closest he'd been to France was making French toast for breakfast.

The thought made me feel a little better.

I stole another peek at my watch. Almost an hour late. A whole hour! I nibbled nervously on my bottom lip, almost forgetting the Pale Amaryllis. *One more minute,* I promised myself silently. *Dad, if you show up this next minute, I'll forgive you for everything.*

The door to the dining room opened. My heart leaped. *Dad!* I thought.

But it wasn't Dad at all. It was only the maître d'. I couldn't remember his name. It was something French and practically unpronounceable. He was short and fat and mostly bald, and he'd combed the few hairs he had left way over his head, which made him look totally ridiculous.

Only the maître d'.

Dad! Get here this minute! I thought, clenching my fists as the seconds ticked off in my head.

The maître d's eyes glanced left and right. He began walking in my direction.

I froze. A terrible idea had just occurred to me. What if something had happened? What if there'd been an accident?

I couldn't breathe. I couldn't even move. All sorts of thoughts ran through my head at once, whizzing around like ants in a big ant colony. Daddy had been in a plane crash. No, a car crash. And as they took him to the hospital to try to repair the damage, he'd told the paramedics to find me at Chez François, and then he'd gone into a coma, and—

I took back every single bad thing I'd ever said
or thought about him. Of course he wouldn't want
to miss a celebration with his only daughter! How
could I have been so foolish? Swaying unsteadily, I
got to my feet. My mouth felt like a block of wood.
"Is he all right?" I cried out.

The maître d' looked down his nose. "*Pardon,
mademoiselle?*"

My head felt ready to explode. "Where's my
dad?" I asked.

"Ah." The maître d's face lit up. "*Mademoiselle*, I
have received a message from Monsieur Fow-lair.
He reports zat he has been delayed by a business
meeting. An er-zhent business meeting."

An er-zhent business meeting? I frowned. Er-
zhent, er-zhent . . . *urgent*. Of course! I took a deep
breath. "A business meeting?" I repeated. My heart
was still beating furiously.

The maître d's eyes seemed to flick past me toward a spot on the wall. "*Oui, mademoiselle.*"

"Oh," I said. I didn't know what to think. What
kind of business meeting could be so urgent that
he'd miss a special dinner with his daughter? "Um—
so when should I expect him?" I asked, feeling very
much like a little kid again.

The maître d' stuck his nose into the air.
"Monsieur Fow-lair will not be here at all," he said
haughtily. "But he say zat you must stay and en-
zhoy yourself. Or-dair whatever you like, and we
will put it on his bill."

"But—" I began.

Too late.

The maître d' was gone.

I sank back into my seat, feeling angrier and angrier. More than that, I felt—what was the word? Betrayed. Totally, one hundred percent betrayed. After a moment my eyes filled with tears, and I didn't even make any effort to wipe them away. The candle flame seemed to change shape. I couldn't read the menu anymore, and I didn't even care.

It wasn't fair.

It just wasn't fair.

I blinked to clear my eyes. In the background, I could see people enjoying their food, talking and having a good time. A family was sitting near the door to the kitchen. I had a hollow feeling in the pit of my stomach, and it wasn't because I was hungry. That family should have been me and Dad. It ought to have been us.

I pressed my hand tightly against my mouth so I wouldn't break down in sobs.

A small white-haired man in tails came by my table, holding a violin. He bowed deeply. "*Mademoiselle?*" he asked.

I considered asking if he knew Johnny Buck's latest hit, "Lonely Forever (For You)," but I decided not to. He probably didn't know anything written after Elvis anyway. "Can you play 'Salty Dog Rag'?" I asked sarcastically.

The violinist frowned. "*Pardon?*"

I waved him away. "Never mind," I said, rolling my eyes.

It had been at least an hour since the violinist had stopped at my table, I thought. Maybe two hours. But I didn't dare look at my watch, afraid that I'd find out it had been only fifteen minutes. A thought was beginning to form in my mind.

Enjoy myself, Dad had said.

By golly, if Dad wanted me to enjoy myself, then I *would* enjoy myself. At his expense, of course.

I snapped my fingers. "Waiter!" I called.

The waiter emerged from the shadows and stood by the table. "*Oui, mademoiselle?*"

I gave him a totally blank stare. "I'll have one of everything," I said.

The waiter started. "What?" he demanded in a voice that didn't sound French at all.

I snickered to myself, but I didn't change my expression. "One of everything," I repeated, running my finger down the menu and handing it back to him with a flourish. "And get a move on. I don't have all night."

"One of—everyzing?" the waiter asked, his accent back in place.

"*Un* of *tout*," I said loudly. I tilted my head to the side and stared at him. "Don't you understand French?"

"One of everyzing," the waiter repeated. "*Bien sûr, mademoiselle.*" He bowed and scurried off.

Ha, I thought, watching him go. But after a moment my grin faded.

It was fun yanking his chain.

But it wasn't as much fun as sitting there with my dad would have been.

I bit my lip again, tasting the Pale Amaryllis, and I adjusted my necklace. Then I folded my hands in my lap as maturely as I could. I tried to tune out the other diners.

A tiny little hope was beginning to rise inside me. Maybe Dad's meeting would be over soon. I'd ordered the food just to get his goat, but now I wasn't sure what to do. I wondered if maybe I should set the food out at home, kind of like a surprise. I imagined Dad coming out of his business meeting, telling a cab driver to put the pedal to the metal so he could get home in time to see his daughter. Then he'd come running in the front door.

And if I had all this food on the table when he came in . . .

Then we could have a quiet celebration. A *real* celebration. Just the two of us. In our own house, at our own dining room table, far from snooty maître d's and dorky waiters.

I nodded slowly. Yeah. That sounded about right. I could see my dad already, smiling at me as we sat at home eating steak au poivre. *You really are growing up, Lila*, he'd say. And I'd smile back and say, *Only the best for us, Dad.*

Yeah . . .

I snapped my fingers again. The waiter material-
ized. "*Mademoiselle?*" he asked.

I gave him a haughty stare. "Put everything in a
doggie bag," I said. "Please."

The waiter's jaw dropped. "Huh?" he asked.
"Everyzing? In a doggie bag?"

I was just positive everyone in Paris said "Huh?"
all day long. "A doggie bag," I said loudly, exagger-
ating the movement of my lips. I pantomimed fill-
ing a bag with food. "In a bag *du chien*," I added.
"*Comprenez-vous?*"

The waiter just stood there, stiff as a board, and
for a moment I didn't think he'd *comprenez-vous'*d
at all. But at last he bent at the waist.

"*Oui, mademoiselle,*" he said with a sigh.

I rubbed my eyes and checked the grandfather
clock in the corner of the dining room. Almost
eleven. But Dad should be back any minute. He
wouldn't miss my special dinner. . . .

I yawned. It had been a long day.

I had set out our finest china all the way around
the table. I'd carefully scraped the meals out of
their Styrofoam containers—can you believe Chez
François still uses Styrofoam?—and put them on
the plates. The foie gras, the duck, the funny-
looking green stuff, even the snails.

And the desserts. Especially the desserts.

I sighed and took a tiny bite of the chocolate
mousse thing in front of me. I knew I should really

wait for Dad, but it was so tempting. I licked my lips, closed my eyes, and swallowed.

Mmm-mmm.

I knew I should probably go ahead and eat dinner. I wasn't sure how much longer I could stay awake. But I wanted to wait. I really, really did.

I took one more small bite of the mousse. Just to tide me over till Dad walked in the door. Then one more, because it looked kind of uneven.

The clock chimed eleven.

I stifled another yawn and glanced around the table. Everything looked perfect. He'd be impressed. *He'll probably say, "What a wonderfully thoughtful daughter I have,"* I thought drowsily. *He'll say, "You're really growing up, Lila." He'll—*

I couldn't help it anymore. I yawned, a humongous yawn that seemed to go on and on forever.

Yup. He'd say all that, and I'd just . . . smile. . . .

"Dad?"

I sat bolt upright in the chair and tried to brush the cobwebs out of my brain. I must have fallen asleep. My mouth felt dry, and my eyes wouldn't focus right. "Dad?" I asked, but my voice didn't sound quite like my own.

"I'm sorry, Lila." It wasn't my father at all. It was Mrs. Pervis, our housekeeper. She was in the doorway bundled in her bathrobe, her hair in curlers the way she always does it before going to bed. I took a quick look around the room. My heart sank.

Dad wasn't there.

"Your father called, dear," Mrs. Pervis said gently. "He had to take a flight to New York. Business."

"Business?" I stared at the grandfather clock. "Mrs. Pervis, it's one o'clock in the morning!"

"I know, dear." Mrs. Pervis yawned.

"Who does business at one o'clock in the morning?" I burst out. It felt as though my whole world was crashing down around me. "How can he be in New York when he's supposed to be—"

To be with me, I wanted to say. But I stopped in the middle of my sentence. I didn't want Mrs. Pervis to know how I felt. After all, she wasn't my mother.

Suddenly I felt totally ridiculous in my fancy dress and my new hairdo. *You should have known,* I scolded myself. *Of course he wasn't coming. Probably never planned to come in the first place.* My eyes filled with tears.

Mrs. Pervis coughed. "Shall I wrap this up?"

I'd forgotten the food. Slowly my eyes traveled from one dish to the next. The snails, the duck, the green stuff.

I wasn't even a little bit hungry.

In fact, the whole idea of French food made me want to barf.

I forced myself to smile at Mrs. Pervis. "Don't bother," I told her. "I think we'll just let it rot." Slowly I stood up. "Good night, Mrs. Pervis," I said, leaving the room without waiting for her to answer.

And I headed up to bed feeling just like an orphan.

Four

"So how was your dinner last night, Lila?" Jessica asked at lunch on Monday.

We (that is, all the Unicorns) were sitting at our special table in the cafeteria, the one we call the Unicorner. We'd like to post a unicorn on the wall behind it, just to let the school know the table is ours. Mandy Miller says that you have to keep everybody aware of your club all the time, or else people will forget about you. She's smart that way. But the principal won't let us.

Another way we show what it means to be a Unicorn is to wear purple. I don't mean we wear *all* purple. That'd be boring, like school uniforms or something. But we try to wear something purple every day. That day, for instance, I had on a pale purple Christina Toscanini scarf.

I should tell you about the other members of the club. Jessica you already know. I guess you could say she's the one with the most creative ideas. Well, maybe *creative* isn't the right word. If a plan sounds totally insane, Jessica probably thought of it. And she'd be the first to tell you so herself.

Ellen Riteman is president of the club. She's not exactly quick on the uptake, if you know what I mean. Not that she's dumb or anything—we wouldn't take anybody in our club who had mush for brains—but she says things that make you wonder what planet she's from. She makes me look smart, if that gives you any idea. But we all like her anyway.

Kimberly Haver is the Unicorn who's most interested in *power*. I don't have anything against bosses; I intend to be one myself someday. But Kimberly doesn't want to wait. And she never lets us forget that she's the oldest one in our group. Still, she's a good person to have on your side. I found *that* out the hard way when I was running for club president against her!

Finally there's Mandy Miller. Mandy is the nicest of all of us. She's almost too good for our club. In fact, she joined the goody-gooders' club, the Angels, a while back. But she saw the light and came back to us (hip hip hurray). She's an expert on vintage clothing. She'd look great in anything, except maybe an old fertilizer bag.

"Yeah, Lila," Kimberly said. She put down her fork

and took a sip of milk. "How was Chez François?"

I'd been hoping no one would ask. "Oh, well," I said with a careless wave of my hand. "Chez François was—you know, Chez François!" I laughed.

"I *don't* know," Ellen said with a sigh. She looked dreamily into space. "I'd love to go there someday. But Mom doesn't have the money, and Dad doesn't have the time."

"Give us details, Lila," Jessica said. "Of *course* Chez François was Chez François! What did you wear? What did you eat?"

"Inquiring minds want to know!" Kimberly snickered.

I could feel myself turning bright red. I swallowed hard. There didn't seem to be any easy way out of this one.

"Oh, it was *so* fantastic!" I lied. I tried to make my eyes sparkle. "Dad admired my hair and my dress— I wore the new purple one with the lace trim—and he said he couldn't believe how incredibly mature I seemed."

"You?" Kimberly curled her lip in disgust.

"Yes, me!" I snapped. Honestly, Kimberly can be *so* aggravating. "People are always noticing how mature I am. Unlike *some* people I know."

"What did you order?" Mandy asked.

"Everything," I said, trying not to think about the food I'd left scattered all over the dining room table. When I'd come downstairs in the morning, it had all disappeared. Mrs. Pervis probably had put it in the refrigerator. She's funny that way. "*Un* of *tout*," I said grandly.

Mandy smiled. "But what was the best?"

"My special dessert," I lied. "Dad had them bake a special cake for me. It said *Congratulations, Lila* across the top. In bright green frosting."

"Green?" Kimberly wrinkled her nose. "Why green?"

"I meant purple," I said quickly. "Of course purple. And, um, the cake was in the shape of an *A*."

"An *A*?" Ellen looked confused. "Doesn't Unicorn begin with a *U*?"

"An *A*," I said patiently, "because that's the grade I got on that math test."

It was strange. I could almost see the cake now. Fluffy white frosting, with the message written in script on the top. On the outside I kept smiling, but on the inside I wished Dad had really given me something like that.

"Hmmm." Kimberly rolled her eyes. "Doesn't exactly sound like your dad, Lila," she said suspiciously.

"I guess you just don't know my dad very well, Kimberly," I said, trying hard to smile.

Nobody criticizes my family and gets away with it. Even if their criticisms are true. I swallowed hard. Maybe Dad wouldn't have ordered me a special cake, but he does do lots of things for me. Like giving me the money for the purple dress and the money for the haircut. . . .

And he gives me a lot of freedom too. That's one way to look at it. Not many men would trust their daughters to eat alone at a fancy restaurant like Chez François.

"My dad made me a cake the other day," Mandy said slowly. "It even worked. Sort of. If you like your cake really crumbly."

"My dad's taking up gourmet cooking, if you can believe it," Ellen said. "He's got three different kinds of food processors, and his whole kitchen counter is covered with slicers and dicers. The other day he made a cake from one of those Asian countries. You know." She frowned. "Albania, or something."

"Albania's in Europe, Ellen," Mandy told her.

"It is?" Ellen raised her eyebrows. "Well, it tasted OK anyway."

"My dad tried to make cookies once," Jessica boasted. "He left out half the flour and melted the butter before he put it in. Then he used baking soda instead of baking powder." She stuck out her tongue. "I mean, ga-ross."

"Well, *my* dad didn't do that," I said bravely. I was annoyed that my friends were horning in on the story of my dad and the cake he didn't get for me. "He let François, the best chef in Sweet Valley, bake it."

Well, it wasn't true—but it should have been true. Now that I thought about it, it was pretty neat to have a father who had deep pockets *and* let me have a long leash. Maybe I could get a shopping spree in Paris out of him. Or a first-class trip to Tahiti for me and all my friends. At least for the ones whose dads would let them. Or maybe—

A party, I thought suddenly. "Hey, guys!" I exclaimed. "How long has it been since the Unicorn Club threw a party—I mean a really *big* party?"

"Too long," Mandy said with a sigh.

"Yeah, it's been, like, *months*," Kimberly said, frowning.

Jessica nodded. "I guess we've just been so busy with other stuff, we haven't been able to show the world what kind of parties we can put on."

"Well, that's about to change," I boasted. "We are going to throw the absolutely most awesome party you ever saw." I could see it now. It would be at my house, with all the finest stuff money could buy. Food, music, decorations. Everybody would be invited. Jimmy too, if I could manage that somehow. And Dad wouldn't care.

At least I *thought* he wouldn't care.

Probably.

"A party?" Ellen's eyes opened very wide. "You mean a Unicorn party?"

"The biggest bash in Unicorn history," I assured her. "We'll do it on, let me see . . ." I tried to visualize my dad's schedule in my head. He'd be gone Saturday, I was almost positive. "Saturday night. And we're going to do it right."

"Cool!" Jessica burst out.

"But Lila, how are we going to pay for—" Mandy

began, when suddenly there was a voice at my shoulder.

"Hey, Lila!" I turned to look. My face fell. Caroline Pearce, the biggest gossip in the middle school, was standing right behind me.

"Hi, Caroline." I sighed. There wasn't any point in talking about a party with Caroline there. It'd be all over school within five minutes, and then what if something went wrong? We'd look totally stupid, that's what. I picked up my tray and started to leave the table. "If you'll excuse me—"

But Caroline blocked my way. "How was your dinner last night, Lila?" she asked.

Was it only my imagination, or had she emphasized the word *dinner?*

I forced a big grin onto my face. "Great!" I said, batting my eyelashes a couple of times for good measure. I poked her in the side with my tray. "Listen, Caroline, I'd love to stay and chat, but I just can't," I fibbed.

"Was it really?" Caroline asked, narrowing her eyes.

I wondered how Caroline knew about my dinner. But then, Caroline knows almost everything—who has a crush on whom, whose parents are breaking up and whose are getting back together again, who threw the watermelon rind in last week's food fight (it was Aaron Dallas, in case you were wondering). Of course she knew about my dinner. "It was wonderful," I said.

"You should try Chez François sometime too."

"Funny you should say that," Caroline said, as if she were speaking to herself. "Because, you know, I was there last night."

"You were *what?*" Black spots spun around before my eyes. I forgot about the party altogether. I couldn't believe what I was hearing!

"Yeah," Caroline said. She scratched her head. "My whole family went to Chez François last night. Special treat."

Her whole family. Great. I felt like slowly sinking to the floor. Maybe I could arrange to have a fatal heart attack right that minute, I thought. Then Caroline would be sorry she'd ever started the conversation. "Oh, you were at Chez *François*," I said with a nervous little giggle. Maybe the bell would ring.

The Unicorner was deathly quiet.

Caroline nodded vigorously. "Yup. And we saw you sitting there all alone. For, like, an hour. You didn't even order or anything. My parents and I were feeling kind of bad for you."

"Oh," I squeaked.

Kimberly's eyes narrowed. "What about the cake your dad had them make for you?" she asked me.

"In the shape of an *A*," Jessica chimed in.

Caroline arched her eyebrows. "I didn't see any cake."

I couldn't believe this. I was being absolutely humiliated in front of my friends. "Um," I said helplessly.

"Nice try, Lila," Ellen snickered. "Where was your dad anyway—in Timbuktu?"

"Albania," Mandy supplied.

Kimberly rolled her eyes. "Probably had a business trip."

Caroline smiled smugly. "And when we left, you were still sitting there, checking your watch every fifteen seconds."

The bell rang, but nobody made any move to get up.

"Oh, you left *early*," I said quickly, trying to sound relieved. "Dad and I just got our times mixed up, that's all."

Kimberly made a noise deep in her throat. "Give it up, Lila."

"But it's true!" I insisted, wishing with all my heart it were. "He got in late, he'd had a long flight, and then his cab hit some traffic outside the airport, but he wouldn't have missed my celebration for the world!" I looked frantically from one friend to the next. "The cake and stuff came later on, after he showed up!"

But deep down I knew I wasn't convincing anybody.

"Guess what I'm doing after school, Lila," Ellie McMillan said proudly.

"Going up to the moon in a big red balloon?" I asked.

Ellie giggled. "Uh-uh. Guess again!"

I pretended to think. "I've got it. You're turning into a beautiful fairy princess," I said, snapping my fingers.

Ellie looked disgusted. "No way!"

In this situation, the best thing to do with four-year-olds like Ellie is to keep guessing dumb things until they finally tell you what they're really doing. "Chasing butterflies?" I asked. "Climbing stoplights? Eating a refrigerator?"

"No, silly!" Ellie said. "We're going to the Dairi Burger for dinner! All three of us! And I'm having french fries!"

I grinned, but I didn't feel like grinning. I knew Ellie would have a great time at the Dairi Burger with her mom and her stepfather. The Dairi Burger isn't much, of course. Not compared to Chez François. But to a little kid like Ellie, the Dairi Burger is probably the next best thing to heaven.

I wasn't sorry that Ellie was going.

I was just jealous because I hadn't gotten to eat with my dad the night before.

Jessica, Elizabeth, and I were at the local day care center, where we spend some of our after-school time volunteering. Ellie is my—I don't know what you would call her; my buddy, I guess. She's a real bundle of energy. She talks all the time, and she's got this smile that just won't quit. I never thought I was the type to want lots of children around, but Ellie's the kind of kid who can change your mind about that.

Ellie tugged on my sleeve. "How long till they come to get me?" she asked.

I checked my watch, remembering how many times I'd done that the previous night. "About an hour."

Ellie stuck out her lip. "Mommy said they might be early."

I nodded. They probably *would* be early. Ellie was just a kid, but she had a mother and a step-father who loved her, who made a big deal out of taking her to the only restaurant they could proba-bly afford. They'd even pick her up early to spend some extra time with her.

And as for me, Lila Fowler, daughter of the rich-est man in Sweet Valley . . . my dad hadn't even bothered to show up.

It wasn't fair.

Ellie grabbed a sheet of paper and some mark-ers. "I'm going to draw a drool," she said, putting her finger to her lips as if it were a big secret.

I frowned. "A what?"

"A drool," Ellie repeated. "You know, a drool? Like a diamond or an emerald?"

"Oh, a *jewel*," I said, trying hard not to laugh. I sat back and watched while Ellie sketched a bright orange blob. Snippets of conversation floated to me from all around the room.

"How did you learn how to tie your shoe?" Jessica was asking a kid near me.

"My daddy taught me," the girl said. There was pride in her voice.

Daddy. I didn't want to think about daddies. I looked in the other direction. Elizabeth was reading a picture book to a child who looked about two. "'And who takes care of you?'" she read from the book.

"My big bwuddah!" the child yelled.

I sighed. I didn't want to hear about big brothers either. I turned to the wall, where a big picture was hanging. The picture was just a bunch of marks in yellow crayon, but a teacher had written a caption in bright red ink: *Me and Grandma Reading a Story Together, by Allison.*

My stomach churned. It wasn't fair. It seemed as though everybody in the entire world had somebody who did things with them. Except for me.

I knew my dad worked hard. I knew I was supposed to be understanding about all the business commitments he had. After all, without his money I couldn't—

"Mommy!" Ellie zoomed through the block corner and flung herself at her mother. "You're here!"

"I'm so glad to see you!" Mrs. McMillan wrapped her arms tightly around Ellie and bounced her up and down.

But I turned away.

Much as I like Ellie, it just plain hurt too much to look.

By the end of my time at the center, I'd made up my mind. I needed to see what other families did.

Families that were different from mine. Even if it was only for a little while.

"Um—guys?" I said a little shyly to Elizabeth and Jessica once we were out the door. "What are you doing now?"

Jessica shrugged. "Going home, I guess."

"It's fried chicken for dinner," Elizabeth said. "We have to help make it." She pretended to gag, but then she grinned. "No, I'm kidding, Lila. It'll be fun. What are you doing?"

"Me?" I waved my hand in the air. "Oh, this and that. You know."

Elizabeth nodded. "And after everything's cleaned up," she added, "then we'll play Pictionary in teams."

"*If* we get our homework done," Jessica grumbled.

Elizabeth laughed. "No problem," she said.

"For you, maybe. Not for me," Jessica said. "But it'll be fun to play the game all together." She made a face. "Just as long as I'm not on Steven's team!"

On Steven's team. I knew there were five Wakefields. "You'll have odd teams," I pointed out.

Jessica rolled her eyes. "*Any* team with Steven on it is an odd team." She elbowed me in the ribs. "Get it?"

I got it, but I didn't want to get it. "I mean, five's an odd number," I explained. Hey, no wonder I aced that math test. "Unless your dad has to work late or something?"

Elizabeth shook her head. "Dad? He'd never miss a family game of Pictionary."

"He'd never miss a family game of anything," Jessica put in. "He'd even play a family game of Sit-Around-the-Living-Room-and-Look-at-Each-Other. He'd love it. As long as there were rules and we kept score."

"Then it'll have to be two versus three," I said, hoping they would catch the hint. "And that's not fair. Maybe I should come on over with you," I added slowly, pretending I'd just sort of thought of that idea.

Elizabeth rubbed her chin. "Hey, yeah." She looked at Jessica, who shrugged. "Would you like to join us, Lila?"

Yes! But I was careful to play it real cool. "Gee, that'd be great," I said, staring off into space as if I were running down my evening in my mind. "Sure, I could do that. Let me just call Dad and tell him I won't be home right away."

Jessica lifted an eyebrow. "Your dad?"

"He's working late tonight," I explained. Which was probably true, after all.

Jessica nodded. "No problem, Lila. We'll wait."

Of course I wouldn't be calling my dad at all. I didn't even know if he was in the country. I'd call Mrs. Pervis.

But the twins didn't need to know that.

And I was too excited about being invited to the Wakefields' to worry about it—much.

Five

Dinner at my house is usually very quiet. Lots of times I'm the only one there. And when Dad does get around to coming home, we just sort of sit and eat. Our conversations go like this:

DAD (chomping): So how was your day, Lila?

ME: Um—fine.

DAD: That's nice.

Then he opens up the newspaper or something. Most of the time, dinner at the Fowlers' is like a silent movie.

Dinner at the Wakefields' is—well, different.

"Pass the chicken," Steven said with his mouth full of corn.

"Pass the chicken, *please*," Mrs. Wakefield reminded him.

"How many pieces have you already had, huh?"

Jessica demanded. She waved her fork in the air. "Five? Six? Twelve?"

"For your information," Steven said, "the nutritional value of chicken is amazingly high. But you wouldn't know that, would you? Pass the chicken, *please*."

"It's all gone," Elizabeth said.

"Oh, for—" Steven rested his elbows on the table. I watched, fascinated. My dad would have told him to get his elbows off the table right away, but no one corrected Steven—or even seemed to notice. "What does a guy have to do to get a decent meal around here?"

"Well, for one thing," Jessica said pointedly, "he could actually help *cook* the dinner now and then. For a change."

Steven took a huge swallow of milk and swished it around in his mouth. "I'm a busy guy. And I do so cook sometimes. Remember that soup I made last week?"

"The one with sesame seeds instead of barley?" Elizabeth asked, suppressing a laugh.

Steven snorted. "Yeah, well, everybody makes mistakes."

"Your quota's filled," Jessica shot back, swallowing. "It was filled when you were, like, *two*. Next time you make a mistake—"

"Fat lot you know," Steven interrupted, wiping his mouth with his sleeve. "Listen, I've got half a mind—"

"For once Steven Wakefield speaks the truth!" Jessica shouted triumphantly. Steven turned red, and Jessica pumped her fists in the air. "Jessica two, Steven nothing!"

"Kids, kids," Mr. Wakefield interjected. "Can't you get along even once at the dinner table?" He motioned to me. "I'm afraid our guest will get the wrong idea about the way our family works."

The wrong idea? As far as I was concerned, this was heaven. The Wakefields had real conversations with each other. They were rude, they argued, they rolled their eyes—and I loved every minute of it.

"The whole trouble with you," Steven said, lifting his fork and pointing it at Jessica as if it were a lethal weapon, "is . . ."

I sighed and leaned back in my chair. I tried to imagine my father and me having this kind of relationship. We'd sit at the dinner table, and the conversation would go something like this:

ME: Hey, Dad, I had such a great day at school! Let me—

DAD: That's great, Li! But listen to what happened at my lunch with the president of Amalgamated Perforating—

ME (louder): Oh, I'm so interested in hearing about it, Dad! But first I want to tell you what Jessica told me—

DAD (holding up his hand): That reminds me, did you hear the story about how we lost the Schimberg account? You're gonna die!

And we'd end up telling every detail of our day.

We'd connect. Just like the Wakefields.

I sighed.

Dream on, Fowler, I told myself, shaking my head.

"Dream on!" Steven was saying disdainfully, practically in my ear. I snapped back to the present. "You did not clear the table last night!"

"Did too," Jessica said loftily. She sat straight up and stared at her brother as if he were from Mars. "Ask anybody."

Steven shook his head so violently I thought it might come off. "I'm talking about *last night*. Remember? We had creamed tuna fish on toast and—"

"That was the night *before* last, Steven," Elizabeth interrupted. "*Last* night was—"

"Was not," Steven snapped.

"*I* did it last night," Jessica argued. "You don't need to be a brain surgeon to know—"

"Talking about *brains*," Steven interrupted, giving Jessica a murderous look.

"It isn't *my* turn anyway," Elizabeth said loudly. "*I* did it on Saturday, just in case anybody is interested."

"It's definitely my turn *tomorrow*," Jessica said frostily. "I know that because—"

"Children!" Mr. Wakefield's voice boomed out across the room. The three kids stopped talking. "I don't care *who* does it," he said slowly, "as long as *somebody* does it. Got it?"

Elizabeth took a deep breath. "But I *distinctly* remember—"

"Well, you're wrong!" Jessica snapped.

"What *both* of you clowns don't understand is that it's not my turn!" Steven said, thrusting his empty plate forward.

I thought about clearing the table myself. I had never cleared a dish before in my life. The idea of doing it myself was kind of weird. After all, that's what waiters are for, right?

Waiters and Mrs. Pervis.

But if I stepped in and did the clearing, how tough could it be? It wouldn't take long, I figured. And if I didn't do it, the twins and Steven might argue till next Thursday. And then we'd never get to Pictionary.

"I'll clear the table, Mr. Wakefield," I said brightly, pushing my chair back and standing up.

"Well!" Mr. Wakefield looked at me, surprised. "Thanks a lot, Lila. What a mature, responsible thing for you to do. You obviously have very good manners."

I bit my lip, pleased to hear so much praise but not sure how to handle it. "Thank you," I murmured, piling up silverware on my plate.

"I'm *telling* you—" Steven said loudly.

"Yeah, right." Jessica made a face.

I decided to start with the plate of corn on the cob. Setting it on the counter, I wondered what to do with the leftovers. Personally, I would have just thrown them out. Who wants to eat cold corn? But Mrs. Pervis would probably have wrapped them up and put them in the refrigerator. I reached for a brown paper grocery bag lying next to the sink.

"Try a plastic one, Lila," Mrs. Wakefield suggested. "Look in the third drawer down."

"One of these days you're going to be sorry you acted like this," Steven threatened. "When I'm President and . . ."

Plastic? I couldn't see why a plastic grocery bag would be better than a paper one. But then, it was Mrs. Wakefield's house. She made the rules. I rooted in the drawer and found a bunch of bags with sealable tops. *Oh, yeah,* I thought. I'd seen them once or twice before. I put the corn into the refrigerator, put the plate in the sink, and turned on the cold water tap full blast.

"Kisser-upper," Jessica hissed at me as I got the empty dish of chicken off the table.

I smiled. "Can I help it if I'm civilized?" I asked.

"Well, you don't have to be so obvious about it," Jessica grumbled.

I put the chicken plate into the sink with the other dirty dishes. I'd never washed a dish, of course. But I knew all about putting dishes in to soak. I'd seen someone do it in the movies once. You can learn an awful lot from the movies if you watch enough of them.

"Um, Lila?" Elizabeth frowned in my direction. "Aren't you going to soak the dishes in hot water instead of cold?"

Oops, I thought, running to change the position of the faucet.

Guess the movies left that part out!

*   *   *

"You may have manners, kid, but you sure can't draw," Steven complained later on that evening.

"Me?" I put my hand against my chest in disbelief. "I won a prize in the first-grade art contest!"

"When was that?" Steven shot back. "Last year?" He held up my drawing for the word *restaurant*. "I can't tell what any of this stuff is!"

We were playing Pictionary. Steven, Jessica, and I were all on a team together. We were losing, but I didn't care. I was having a blast.

"Maybe you need your eyes checked, Steven," Mrs. Wakefield suggested. "Lila, why don't you explain?"

"It's totally obvious," I said, pointing to the first picture. "It's a kid taking a nap, duh. He's a rester, right? And this thing with six legs is an ant. A two-year-old would know that. *Rester-ant; restaurant*, get it?"

Steven grimaced. "Are you kidding? The first picture looks like a toad with a machine gun, and the second—" He squinted.

"Steven," Mr. Wakefield said warningly. "Lila's our guest. See if you can stop picking on her."

"Ah, forget it," Steven muttered.

But I didn't mind at all. I really didn't. In fact, I liked Steven's teasing. I was being treated like a member of the family. As though I belonged.

I sighed and leaned back against the couch. I could almost imagine Steven being my own big brother, the protective, helpful big brother I didn't have. There'd be this big guy bugging me outside the mall, and Steven would show up just in time. . . .

STEVEN *(wrapping his arm tightly around me):* Hey, you! Beat it. Leave my sister alone.

BIG GUY: *All right already! (He disappears.)*

STEVEN *(patting me on the back): Just let me know if he tries that stuff on you again, OK, kiddo?*

I nodded. It sounded just about right. Only then maybe Jimmy Lancer would appear, and . . .

JIMMY *(awkwardly): Hey, um, Lila?*

ME: *Yes?*

JIMMY *(clearing his throat): Um, well, I was watching Steven be so protective of you just now and, um, I—*

ME *(smiling): Go on.*

JIMMY *(quickly): I was just realizing how incredibly special you are, Lila.*

I took a deep breath. Jimmy would lean closer, and his eyes would be like liquid pools, and my heart would be beating fast, and our lips would be just about to meet, and—

"Lila!"

Startled, I looked up. Steven was standing in front of me, waving his hand in front of my eyes.

"Hello? Lila?" he demanded. "Like, it's your *turn?*"

I blushed more furiously than ever. And my fantasy came crashing down around me. It wasn't true, wouldn't ever come true. Steven wasn't my big brother at all. He was just a high-school kid who thought I was a pain.

I didn't belong there, I realized. Steven teased

his sisters because deep down he really liked them. But he teased me because I was a pest. Lila the doofus, that was me. I couldn't even draw a stupid *ant*. I couldn't concentrate on the game I'd wanted so badly to play. I—

I shook my head. "I think I should probably be getting home," I said in a flat voice, trying to keep my emotions under control.

Mrs. Wakefield frowned and looked at her watch. "My goodness, it *is* late! We'll give you a ride, dear. Your dad must be wondering where you are."

I decided not to say that my father was probably halfway around the world. Or that he didn't even know where I was to begin with. Or that he had better things to do than worry about his only daughter anyway. I found my backpack and jacket. "Thanks for everything," I said softly.

"You're very welcome," Mrs. Wakefield said breezily. "We're glad to have you, Lila. You're almost like a member of the family!"

I forced a grin onto my face, but my heart was heavy. *Almost* didn't quite cut it.

I tried not to think of my dark, gloomy, empty house.

"Come again," Mr. Wakefield said with a smile.

I nodded. But I didn't think I would.

It was just too painful to be around a real family.

Six

I came downstairs slowly the next morning, clutching my purple bathrobe tightly around me. I was hoping I'd misjudged my dad. The previous night had been pretty terrible, but that morning things somehow seemed better.

I guess mornings will do that to you.

Of course Dad loves you, I told myself, feeling a little more cheerful. *He just shows it in a different way than Mr. and Mrs. Wakefield.* And dinner at Jessica's house had been kind of—well, messy. Chaotic.

I put a grin on my face and marched into the dining room. Then I stopped short.

"Dad!"

I stood in the doorway, staring in surprise. My father was there, sitting at the table in his power tie and his fancy silk suit, reading the business pages of the *Los Angeles Times*.

Dad glanced up. "Good morning, Lila," he said, flashing me a quick smile before he disappeared behind the newspaper.

"I—I didn't know you were home," I said.

Dad shrugged. "Took the red-eye last night," he said with a yawn. "Got back about three A.M."

"Oh." Slowly I sat down in the chair opposite his. The newspaper rustled. "Didn't you come upstairs to say hi?" I asked, giving a little laugh to let him know it was a joke.

Dad's a little lacking in the humor department.

He flipped to another page and ran his eye down the columns. "No, sweetie," he said in a bored voice. "It was awfully late, and I knew you needed your sleep."

Like I said.

But I was a little offended that Dad hadn't at least checked on me. Some fathers like to do that, you know. If they get home late from a business trip, they check on their children and make sure they're OK.

"I was just joking, Dad," I said, reaching for the cereal. There was silence.

I wanted him to apologize for Sunday night. I wanted him to say he felt horribly guilty and to ask how he could make it up to me. I wondered why he wasn't saying anything. "Dad?" I asked.

Rustle, rustle. There was a faint sigh from across the table. "Yes, Lila?"

I looked down at my empty plate. "Nothing," I muttered.

There was silence again. Silence so loud I could almost hear it. When Dad turned to another page of the financial news, it sounded like a rifle shot.

I bit my lip. *Apologize,* I thought, concentrating on sending thought waves to Dad. Although I have to admit he wouldn't be the type to have ESP. *Apologize. . . .*

Dad cleared his throat. "Oh, Lila?"

My heart leaped. "Yes?" I asked.

Dad rattled his coffee cup. "Please pass the butter."

The butter. Oh. Without a word I picked up the silver butter dish and banged it down next to his arm. Then I grabbed the box of cereal and tore it open as roughly as I could.

Dad didn't even look up.

My shoulders slumped. I didn't think I was asking for so much. An apology. A promise that he'd never stand me up again. A little attention.

Even a *very* little attention would do, I thought.

I tore off the top of the cereal box and dropped it onto the floor. Next I poured way too much cereal into my bowl and drowned it in milk. Still Dad didn't move. At last I picked up a fork, thrust it into my cereal bowl, and dragged the tines across the bottom of the bowl till they shrieked. *Ugh!* I covered my ears and looked hopefully at my father.

He lowered the paper and frowned. "Something wrong, dear?"

"Wrong?" I scowled. "Nothing's wrong." Then, as he nodded and started to turn back to the news, I added quickly: "It's just that—that—"

My lower lip quivered. Rats! I wanted to sound angry, but I was more sad than mad. "It's just that you were going to take me to dinner at Chez François because of my A," I said in a very small voice.

"Oh, that." Dad waved his hand in the air. "Didn't you get my message?"

I nodded, not trusting myself to speak.

Dad sat back and smiled. "Then it was all right, wasn't it?" he said cheerfully. "I'm sure you had a very nice meal. It isn't every girl who gets to eat at Chez François, you know."

I licked my lips and twisted my napkin forlornly in my lap, remembering Caroline Pearce and her family. "But—" I began. Tears stung my eyes, and I wished he would understand.

Dad sighed. "I'm really, really proud of that A you got in science. I want you to know that."

"In math," I corrected him, staring at my over-flowing bowl.

"Sure, math." Dad's eyes flicked disapprovingly to the milk dripping onto the tablecloth. "And I know you wanted me there Saturday night."

Sunday, I thought, not even bothering to say it out loud.

Dad coughed. "But sweetie, you know how it is."

I nodded again. I knew how it was. Business

would always come first, and I would be way back in second place.

Dad reached into the pocket of his jacket and brought out his wallet. "I know you're disappointed, baby, but maybe this will help," he said softly.

One by one Dad pulled out five crisp bills and handed them to me. I stared. Five twenty-dollar bills, hot off the presses. The serial numbers were in order and everything. "But—" I began.

Dad cut me off. "Buy yourself something nice," he said.

Zip! Up went the paper again.

I took a deep, shivery breath and wrapped the bills inside my fist. Money? How would this prove that he loved me? The week before, maybe it would have. But now I wasn't so sure. Now I wanted two tickets to a concert, one for me and one for him. Or a gift certificate good for a walk in the woods. Or even—

I sighed. What I really wanted, I realized, was for him to reschedule the dinner. I needed a dad— not a personal banker.

Slowly I raised my head. "Dad?" I asked tentatively. Maybe we could make a date for another time.

The newspaper rustled impatiently.

"Not now, sweetheart," came Dad's voice from somewhere behind it. "I'm busy."

"So about this party that Lila was talking about yesterday," Ellen said at lunch.

I nodded. The more I thought about a party, the more sense it made. Dad had as good as told me that I didn't need much parenting. It was OK for me to do what I wanted. And he was giving me money right and left. "I think—" I began.

"The most important question is," Kimberly interrupted, "what kind of decorations to have. I nominate myself for decorations chair." She stared hard at Ellen.

"I second the nomination," Ellen said quickly.

"Decorations aren't important," Jessica jumped in. "Not yet anyway. The real key is going to be the music. We should find the most totally radical group we—"

Mandy shook her head. "Actually, the first thing to consider is the marketing plan, especially if the party's going to be on Satur—"

"Purple and white streamers to start with, of *course*," Kimberly said loudly.

"Because if we have a party and no one hears about it—" Mandy was saying.

"Does anybody know a band called Dutch Elm Disease?" Jessica demanded. "My brother says they stink, so it's probably worth—"

"We'll drop a big purple ball," Kimberly went on, her eyes shining. "Just like in Times Square at midnight on New Year's Eve. But our parents probably won't let us stay out that late, so we can do it at ten-thirty—"

"How about food?" Ellen asked. "I think we ought to serve—"

Jessica and Kimberly opened their mouths. "Of course, it all depends on the size of the room," they said at the exact same moment, and turned to look at each other in alarm.

Just the moment I'd been waiting for. "Hey, guys!" I said, raising my voice so I would be heard. "It won't be just the party of the decade; it'll be the party of the century. Because, you see, I'm volunteering my place."

It made perfect sense. This would be my chance to show the Unicorns how tight I was with Jimmy. I'd invite him, I decided. The idea was exciting. I'd tell him to come a little early, while we were setting up. My friends would be absolutely floored when he came in and kissed me.

And my dad wouldn't mind. No. He wouldn't mind at all.

"Hey, yeah!" Ellen turned to me, a big smile on her face.

"Awesome!" Jessica thrust both fists in the air. "Big enough for any band at all. Think we could get the Buckster?"

"What a place for decorations," Kimberly muttered, her lips curving up into a grin.

"How about money?" Mandy asked with a frown. "Last time I looked, we had, like, twelve dollars and thirty-six cents in the treasury. Plus a couple of pizza delivery coupons."

"Oops," Ellen said, wrinkling her nose.

"Details," I said. "We'll think of some kind of

fund-raiser. And if not—" I paused, knowing I really shouldn't be bankrolling my friends. But this way I could impress Jimmy and the Unicorns at the same time. And more important, this was a chance to see just how far I could push my dad.

"If we can't raise enough ourselves," I said, "then the party's on me."

"All right!" Kimberly cried. Ellen applauded, and Jessica gave me a standing ovation, all by herself.

On my dad, really, I thought mischievously as my friends calmed down. *Whether he knows it or not!*

"Come on, guys, let's hit the mall!" I said.

School was over for the day, and the hundred bucks Dad had given me that morning was burning a hole in my pocket. Excuse me, in my *purse*. I decided I'd spend the cash on something good. New jewelry, maybe, or a designer sweatshirt.

I looked around at the other Unicorns. We were standing in the hallway by Jessica's locker. No one said a word. "Guys?" I repeated.

"I can't," Ellen said brightly. "My mom and I are planting a new garden. We're doing it together. Like, a mother-daughter project."

"Cool," Mandy said.

"It's going to be fun," Ellen added. "And if we do really well, I mean *really* well, we win a prize from Mom's garden club."

"Oh, wow," I said sarcastically. "What do you win? Like, three bags of fertilizer?"

Ellen frowned. "Two bags, I think," she said.

"I have to get home early today," Kimberly said. "We're going to my cousin's for dinner."

"Which cousin?" Jessica wanted to know. "The really dreamy tall guy you're going to introduce me to someday soon?" She dug her elbow into Kimberly's ribs.

Kimberly shook her head and made a face. "Nope. The dippy fifteen-year-old girl who thinks I'm a little kid. 'How's *middle school*, Kimberly?' she says every time she sees me."

"You should just say, 'Great! How's *lower school* going for you?' " Jessica suggested.

Kimberly grinned. "Maybe I will."

"Jessica?" I asked. I was sure I could count on Jess. We'd have fun, I thought. Even if it was just the two of us, checking out dresses and accessories and stuff. I put my arm around her shoulder. "You're coming, of course."

Jessica's mouth was a tight line. "I wish," she said. "But Steven's got a basketball game, so I have to go and cheer."

"Oh." My face fell.

"You'd cheer for Steven?" Ellen asked doubtfully.

Jessica snorted. "No way. I'm cheering for the other team. Whoever they are."

I plastered my biggest, best smile on my face. "Well, Mandy," I said heartily, "looks like it's you and me."

"I'd love to come with you, Lila," Mandy said.

"But I have to baby-sit my little brother." She rolled her eyes. "Sorry."

She wasn't half as sorry as I was.

"Well, all right," I said. I stepped toward the door. "If no one cares about upholding the honor of the Unicorns anymore, well . . ." I paused to give them a chance to change their minds.

Mandy smiled. "You mean 'To shop or not to shop, that is the question,'" she quoted. "I'd like to think that this club has moved a little beyond that."

"Yeah, Lila," Kimberly put in.

"I was just—" I began. But I saw I couldn't win. "See you around," I said, half under my breath, and I turned and flounced down the hall.

I'd been abandoned by my dad, and now I'd been abandoned by my friends, even if they *had* liked the idea for the party. I wandered sadly around the mall, tightly clutching my purse. I'd been so desperate for company, I'd even stopped on my way out of the building and asked Evie Kim and Mary Wallace if they wanted to come with me. Evie and Mary used to be Unicorns, but now they belong to the Angels. That's how low I'd sunk.

They couldn't make it, of course. Evie had to practice her violin for some recital that night. Her relatives were coming, naturally. And I didn't hear Mary's excuse, but I was totally positive it was because she had to spend time with her family.

I was so sick of hearing that expression. Especially since I didn't have much of a family to spend time with.

I walked on past the shoe store and the sportswear boutique. Everything looked boring. The jewelry at Sweet Valley Jewelers wasn't my style. The dresses at Two Fashion Place looked like cheap imitations of Belle da Costa designs. Feeling incredibly sorry for myself, I walked into Totally Hip, the music store that's so hip its name doesn't even tell you what it sells, and started flipping through the racks of CDs.

Totally Hip wasn't very interesting either. Looking at Johnny Buck CDs didn't exactly compare to attending his last concert. Which I had. In London. Next to that, a row of recordings didn't amount to much. I was about to leave the store when I glanced up and saw Jimmy Lancer.

My heart skipped a beat. Yes, it really did! Hardly able to breathe, I made my way over to where he was standing. *Maybe it's fate,* I thought. It was just meant to be. Me and Jimmy. Jimmy and Lila.

He was in the hard rock section, pawing through the racks, and he didn't notice me.

I stepped closer and picked up a CD from the bin. "Oh, yeah, the—um—Mangy Muttheads," I said aloud, straining to read the print on the front. I tried hard to get the right number of exclamation marks into my voice. "That band's to die for!"

Jimmy turned around. "Hey, Lila!" he said happily.

"What are you doing here? Didn't know you were a metal fan."

I wasn't, but Jimmy didn't have to know that. "Oh, yeah." I grinned. "These guys are, you know, some of my favorites."

Jimmy nodded vigorously. "They're wicked," he agreed. "It's just too bad their stuff is so expensive in the U.S."

"It is?" I couldn't help asking. "I mean, yeah, it sure is," I corrected myself. I squinted down at the price sticker. Twenty-five dollars. It did seem a little steep for a CD with only five songs on it.

I stole a quick look at Jimmy. *He is so cool*, I thought. I especially liked his grin. It was so confident. Not one of those lopsided, embarrassed-little-boy grins that the kids in my grade all have.

I wondered if maybe I did have a shot at him. He was older, yeah, but still, he *was* smiling right at me.

And he *had* acted glad to see me.

I stepped closer, so that anybody walking by might think we were, you know, a couple.

"Yeah," Jimmy was saying. He wrinkled his nose. He was even cute when he wrinkled his nose. "It's just that the Mangy Muttheads record in England."

I nodded as if I'd known that since age two. And suddenly I had a brilliant idea. I swung my purse off my shoulder. "Let me buy it for you," I offered, smiling broadly.

"Buy it? For me?" Jimmy stepped back, blinking

in surprise. Then he grinned. "Oh, yeah," he said with a laugh. "Sure thing."

"I'm serious," I said. "Really. I just—um—came into some money, and, um, I'd be honored if you'd let me buy it for you." I moved a step forward. Did I dare let my arm kind of casually rest on his?

I decided I didn't.

Jimmy shoved some stray hair out of his eyes. He shook his head. "No thanks. Really. I'd love to have it, but I just can't accept a gift like that." He held up his hands. "But thanks. I mean it, Lila."

I frowned. Maybe I was coming on too strong. "Please? It's just that I, um—" I thought hard. "That I love this music so much," I lied, "and I like to help people who have the same taste as I do!" I grinned at him, but this time I was grinning in a way that I hoped wasn't too romantic.

Not that I didn't want to be romantic. It's just— well, you know.

Jimmy hesitated. "Twenty-five dollars," he muttered. "That's a lot for a CD."

"No problem," I said. "Let's make a pile!" Quickly I grabbed three more CDs and put them on top of the Mangy Muttheads disc. Then I stepped back and smiled. "They're yours, Jimmy."

Jimmy's jaw dropped. "No. No way," he said, but he reached forward and thumbed through the CDs.

I stood still and waited.

"Gee, look at that," Jimmy mumbled under his breath. "The Houston concert of the Slashed

Shin Guards! I thought that one hadn't been re-
leased because of the riot."

The riot? I made a face.

Jimmy gave me a shy smile. "OK, Lila," he said.
"If you insist."

I scooped up the CDs before he could change his
mind and headed for the checkout. "I insist!" I said
happily.

"You're really something else," Jimmy said as he
caught up with me. He draped an arm casually
around my shoulder. I almost stopped breathing.
"Good thing I ran into you!"

I smiled my best smile, feeling the pressure of
his arm against my neck. "You've got it backward,
Jimmy," I told him. "Good thing *I* ran into *you!*"

Seven

"Have some salad, Lila," Mrs. Pervis said.

It was Tuesday night, and Dad and I were having dinner together.

Well, we were at the same table anyway.

"Thanks, Mrs. Pervis," I said, taking the bowl from her. But I had no appetite. "Dad?" I asked.

I'd been thinking all day long. And I'd decided I really needed to tell him about Jimmy. Now that we were practically dating and everything, I really needed Dad's permission to be going out at all. Especially in this case, because Jimmy was so much older than me.

"Just a minute, honey," Dad murmured.

I sighed as Mrs. Pervis left the room and shut the door firmly behind her. Dad had arrived at the table with a humongous briefcase. He'd plonked it down next to his plate and opened it without even bothering to say hello. Since then he'd been shuffling papers and not paying attention to me at all.

I stared down into my salad bowl. Arugula, radicchio, and romaine mixed with scallions. Not your average salad, but then this wasn't your average dinnertime either.

Did I say dinnertime at the Fowlers' was like a silent movie? Well, I take it back. It was more like a painting: *Still Life of Father and Daughter*.

I bit my lip. I was determined to talk to Dad no matter what. "Dad?" I asked brightly. "Would you tell me about your company?"

It was worth a try. Maybe he'd get interested in talking about it, since running the company took up so much of his time. Then I could just kind of casually work in Jimmy.

Dad looked up, a puzzled expression on his face. "Fowler Enterprises?" he asked. He cleared his throat. "Well, dear, I do importing and exporting. And a whole lot more." He turned back to his papers.

I tried again. "Do you use, you know, computers?"

Dad looked up, a smile frozen on his face. "Computers, honey?" he asked. "Tons. We're a leader in systems technology, especially where the new modem port start-ups are concerned. The terminals all interface with one another using the BBB triple-megabyte system log." His pen moved quickly across the page in front of him. "Clear?"

"Um—yeah," I said slowly. Clear as mud anyway. "But—"

Dad pulled a cell phone out of his briefcase. "That can't be right," he muttered to himself, punching in a number.

I sat in my seat, feeling as ignored as the lettuce leaves in my salad bowl.

"Mr. Lum?" Dad said into the receiver. "Yeah, Fowler here. Listen, I'm reviewing the notes from Friday's meeting, and I've found some amounts that don't jibe. . . ."

More business. I massaged my cheeks. *He doesn't mean to ignore me*, I told myself. If he knew how I felt, he'd stop.

At least I was almost positive he would.

"All right," Dad said into the receiver. "Talk to you later, then." He snapped the phone off and set it in his briefcase. Then he went back to work.

My mouth felt dry for no particular reason. "So, um, Dad?" I asked.

"Uh-huh," Dad said absently, not looking up from his papers.

I swallowed hard. It was now or never. And, like Shakespeare or another one of those guys said, honesty is the best policy. "Well, I met this *guy*," I said, emphasizing the last word in case Dad wasn't listening too hard. "And he's a real fox."

Dad made a mark with his pen.

I wished I could get in between him and the paper. "I think I'm—um—interested," I said. "And I think he is too."

In the movies, when daughters make announcements like that, sometimes the parents are thrilled and other times they're totally bummed. Either way, they notice. But that's the movies, I guess. Dad still didn't look up. "That's nice, dear," he said pleasantly.

I bit my lip. I suspected that I could have said, *Hey, Dad! The house is on fire!* and he would still have said, *That's nice, dear.* I resisted the urge to wave my hand in front of his face and say, *Earth to Dad!*

"And not only that—" I went on, but at that moment the cell phone shrilled.

Dad looked at me long enough to put a warning finger to his lips. He scooped up the phone. "Fowler," he said. Then he paused. "Oh, hello, Long. Are the blueprints ready yet? By Saturday? Make it Friday and we've got a deal."

Mrs. Pervis held out a plate of steamed clams toward me. I was getting kind of steamed myself; I hadn't even seen her come in. I shook my head.

"Are you sure?" she mouthed at me.

"I'm sure," I whispered back. Mrs. Pervis sighed, set a plate of clams in front of Dad, and left the room.

"Friday, then," Dad said, and he hung up. Back he went to his work. I saw that he hadn't touched his salad either.

"Dad," I said, "I really, really want you to meet this guy." I tried to make eye contact. "I want you to make sure he's, you know, right for me."

I hoped my voice had at least a hint that maybe this guy *wasn't* quite right for me.

"Because you might not approve of him," I added quickly.

Dad glanced up. "Oh, I trust your judgment, dear."

"You do?" The words were out of my mouth before I realized what I was saying. "I mean— that's nice. I guess."

I looked down at my wilting salad.

It wasn't nice at all.

Dad didn't really mean that he trusted my judgment. He was just saying that he couldn't be bothered.

I thought about throwing my salad across the table. That would get his attention, all right. Or standing up on my chair and yelling, "This guy I'm trying to tell you about? He's twenty-eight years old and has been in jail six times!" But I didn't.

Dad reached for his cell phone again and started to punch in another number.

I took a deep breath.

I'd get Dad's attention, I promised myself. Somehow . . .

"I'm telling you, we've been out a couple of times," I told the other Unicorns at lunch on Wednesday. Mrs. Pervis had packed me a container of sole amandine, which certainly looked better than Mandy's peanut butter and banana sandwich.

"No possible way!" Kimberly scoffed.

"I'm telling you the truth," I lied. I batted my eyelashes to show that there was more to my relationship with Jimmy than they thought. "We went to Casey's, we went to the zoo—" I ticked places off on my fingers. "And then we just sat on one of the park benches for *hours*." I winked at Ellen.

"You didn't!" Ellen said.

"We did so," I told her. I spread out my hands. "We may not be ready for a write-up in the *National Whisperer* yet, but this is going to be one of those torrid romances you read about."

Jessica snorted. "You lied to us about your dad meeting you for dinner, Lila. Why should we believe you about this?"

I felt my cheeks turn pink. "Jessica, I'm surprised at you!" I shot back. "I lied about my dad because—well, because. But I'm not lying about Jimmy. This one happens to be true."

Kimberly gave me a look. "Proof, Lila."

"Proof?" I thought fast. "I just so happen to have a date with him for this Friday night."

"What?" Mandy sat up straight.

"Dream on," Kimberly muttered. But she didn't sound as sure as she'd sounded a minute before.

"Seriously?" Jessica narrowed her eyes. "You're joking, right?"

"No way," I told them. "I have a date for Friday night with Jimmy Lancer."

It sounded great. And maybe if I said it enough times, it would come true.

"Where?" Ellen wanted to know.

"Um—" I searched my mind. What would impress them? "At—at Chez François," I said at last.

Mandy whistled. "Who's paying, I'd like to know?"

I gave her a piercing look. "None of your business," I told her. Getting a reservation wouldn't be a problem, I reminded myself. François always keeps a table for Dad, just in case. The only hard part would be getting Jimmy.

The only hard part. Yeah, sure.

Well, I'd think of something.

Kimberly's frown deepened again. "I don't know," she said slowly. "I saw Jimmy at the Dairi Burger the other night with Hilary Smithwick."

I tried not to act surprised. Hilary, I knew, was one of the more popular girls at Sweet Valley High. "Oh, *Hilary*," I said, tossing my head carelessly. "I think she and Jimmy, like, grew up together."

But I began to wonder. *What if—no. Not after the way Jimmy looked at me.*

"I still don't believe it," Jessica said, shaking her head. "Let's face it, Lila—Jimmy may be cute and all, but he's in high school. No way is your dad letting you go out with an older guy."

"Yeah." Ellen nodded. "My dad would *never* let me."

"Mine either," Mandy agreed.

I turned to face Jessica. "You're just plain wrong," I told her. "I can do whatever I want, and my dad doesn't care."

"But—" Ellen started to say.

"Love is love, right?" I interrupted. "If a guy is right for you, he's right for you, no matter how old. My dad says he trusts my judgment. I don't have to follow silly rules like you guys."

"Ouch!" Kimberly pretended to rub her cheek. "Cheap shot, Lila."

"But true." I smiled.

Jessica shook her head. "Your dad really doesn't care who you go out with?"

"He doesn't care," I said. And then more forcefully, I repeated it. "My dad doesn't care."

But deep down something was nagging me. I couldn't help thinking about my dinner at the Wakefield house. They had rules. And they also had love and affection and togetherness.

I didn't have rules. That was for sure. But I didn't really have love or togetherness either.

My dad didn't even care whom I was dating.

Usually I don't have much trouble making a phone call. If I have to call up a friend for a homework assignment, no problem. If I have to call the salon to set up an appointment, I can do it in two seconds. And if somebody gives me terrible service, I'm on the phone like *that*.

But this call was different.

I stared at the phone book lying open in front of me. The number for the Lancer family was circled in bright red ink.

I reached for the phone for about the eighteenth time. But I jerked my hand back.

Part of me wanted my dad to come in and say, *You're dating a kid in high school?* Then maybe he'd rip the phone out of the wall and ground me for a week for having such silly ideas.

And let's face it, I told myself glumly, *it* is *a silly idea.* What would a guy like Jimmy see in a kid like me?

I stared at the phone. Might as well get it over with. What would be the worst that could happen? He'd say, *No, I'm busy, thanks very much.*

Or . . . I licked my lips. No. The worst that could happen would be that he'd say, *A date? With you?* And he'd burst out laughing and hang up the phone.

Or maybe, I thought, the worst thing that could happen would be that he'd actually say yes.

But I didn't want to think about that just then.

Taking a deep breath, I punched in the number before I could change my mind. The phone rang twice—three times. My heart leaped. Maybe no one was home. Maybe they didn't have an answering machine. Maybe I was off the hook. I could always lie to the other Unicorns about my "big date." It was pretty silly to even *think* about inviting him to this party anyway. And maybe it was better not to provoke my dad, just in case he really did care about my dating an older guy—

"H'lo?"

The voice was muffled. Startled, I almost dropped the phone. "Um—hello," I said cautiously. "May I please speak to—"

"Talk a little louder," the voice ordered. Music was playing in the background, I realized. If you could call it music. Somebody was howling at the top of their lungs, and there didn't seem to be any chords or anything—just noise.

"Um—all right," I said, raising my voice a little. This wasn't going very well. "I'd like to speak to Jimmy, please."

"This is Jimmy," the voice replied. "Who's this?"

I gripped the receiver tightly. Jimmy! "Hi," I said. "Um, this is Lila."

There was a pause. The singer in the background hit an especially earsplitting high note. "Huh?" Jimmy asked.

I closed my eyes and opened them again. "Lila," I explained. "Lila Fowler." *The prettiest girl at Sweet Valley Middle School*, I wanted to say, but I decided I'd better not. I gripped the phone tighter than ever. "The one who bought you all those CDs yesterday."

"Oh, Lila!" Jimmy said enthusiastically. "Hey, how you doing, kiddo? I love those albums," he went on without waiting for an answer. "One of them's playing now. Listen!"

Jimmy must have held the phone out toward his speakers, because the music suddenly got louder. I grimaced. *If this is hard rock,* I thought, *I'll take soft pebbles, thanks very much.* Luckily, Jimmy was back on the line a second later. "What's up?" he asked. His voice was friendly, like always.

I swallowed hard. "Um—I was wondering," I began. I wasn't used to asking boys on dates, especially not cute, older guys like Jimmy. I paused. "You, ah, wouldn't like to go to Chez François with me on Friday night, would you?" Somehow that hadn't come out right. "I mean—"

"Chez François?" Jimmy burst out. "That's, like, the most expensive restaurant in town!"

"Oh, I wouldn't expect you to pay," I assured him. "It's on my dad. He wanted to give me a present. You know, a meal there with a friend." *Should I say "a very special friend"? Better not.* "And I chose you!" I finished.

There was silence, except for the Mangy Muttheads in the background. "We'd pick you up around seven," I added faintly.

"We?" Jimmy asked. "You mean you and your dad?"

"Oh, no!" *Dad wouldn't come anyway—even if I asked him to,* I thought hollowly. "No, me and my chauffeur, Richard," I explained.

"Your *chauffeur?*" Jimmy laughed. "Lila Fowler, you sure are something else."

My heart beat faster. "So will you come?" I asked.

I could practically hear Jimmy grinning on the other end of the phone. "Oh, what the heck," he said happily. "Sure, Lila. I'll see you Friday. And thanks for the invite."

I clutched the phone, suppressing a shriek of delight.

I'd done it.

I had a date with the cutest guy in town. At the nicest restaurant in town. Just like I'd told the Unicorns.

I grinned. If I played this right, I'd get my dad's pants full of ants.

And have a little fun in the bargain.

Eight

"So how about that hot date of yours tomorrow, Lila?" Kimberly asked. Her eyes gleamed like a cat's, as if she were about to pounce on me.

It was after school on Thursday, and the Unicorns were at a meeting at Ellen's. At Ellen's mom's, I should say, now that she has two houses. I smiled at Kimberly. A killer smile.

"Oh, we're still on, Kimberly," I said sweetly. "Jimmy called last night and said he could hardly wait."

Of course, he hadn't called me at all; I'd called him. And he'd said "What the heck," not "I can hardly wait." You and I know that. But Kimberly didn't.

"No way!" Kimberly said scornfully.

I spread out my hands. "You don't have to believe it," I said. "But it's true. Jimmy and I are going to Chez François tomorrow night."

Jessica shook her head. "That's so cool," she said. "I'm just shocked that your dad would let you date a guy in high school."

"Like I said," I told her, "my dad trusts my judgment."

"Must be nice," Mandy said. "I know my dad would hit the roof."

"Mine too," Jessica agreed. "I can see it now. He'd say, 'You want to do *what?*'" She shook her head. "I admire you, Lila. You're lucky to be able to pull this off."

I *was* lucky. Jimmy was cute and sensitive and all those other things I look for in a guy. It would have been terrible if Dad hadn't let me take him to Chez François.

Still, it would have been nice if Dad had at least noticed. Maybe he would have blown his stack over Jimmy's age. But then maybe he could have gotten to know Jimmy a little bit and made an exception, just this once, because Jimmy's so cool.

And because I was getting to be so mature and independent.

Yeah. None of the other Unicorns' dads would have seen it like that.

"Well, my dad would be on the warpath too," Ellen said. "But as president of this club, I move that we stop talking about Lila and start talking about parties." Her eyes gleamed. "Like the totally wicked party we're throwing on Saturday."

"Which is in just two days," Mandy sighed.

"Which is exactly why we need to start talking about it now," Kimberly butted in. "All in favor of changing the subject from Lila to the awesomest party of the decade, say aye."

I was a little bummed about changing the subject away from me, but I said aye along with the others.

"Decorations: check," Kimberly said importantly. "My committee's been working on them night and day. Food?"

Mandy shrugged. "We ordered some chips and soda and stuff like that."

"Good," Kimberly said. "Music?"

"I'm afraid I've got some bad news," Jessica said. She looked glum. "Dutch Elm Disease can't make it, so we're without a band."

"Well, that's OK." Mandy shrugged. "With Lila's house, our guests won't even notice."

"Yeah, we'll be so busy swimming in the pool and dancing through the ballroom, no one will care," Ellen agreed.

"Dancing to what, doofus?" Kimberly demanded.

"We'll just crank up some CDs," Jessica said. "Lila's dad has the greatest stereo system. And he won't mind if we use it. Right, Lila?"

"Right," I said slowly.

But I was getting cold feet. The knot that had been in my stomach all week long was getting bigger and bigger. *This is for real*, I thought. *This is getting serious.*

I bit my lip. What if my dad came home early from his trip? What if the party got out of control? What if

Dad saw me and Jimmy together—maybe even kissing?

I shivered.

You wanted this to happen, a little voice in my head reminded me. And I *had* wanted it to happen; that was perfectly true. I hated the way my dad ignored me. And I loved being with Jimmy—and feeling his hand in mine.

I took a deep breath. *It will be fun*, I assured myself, trying to calm my butterflies.

"Place? Lila?" Kimberly's eyes narrowed.

"Check," I said quickly.

"Did you talk to your dad?" Jessica wanted to know.

I shrugged. "Not exactly. But I don't really need to." I studied my fingernails intently.

Mandy shook her head. "I hate to be a party pooper, but shouldn't you clear it with him first, Lila?" she asked. "What if he says no about using the house?"

"He won't say no," I assured Mandy, not looking at her. "He thinks I'm mature and responsible and can make my own decisions." Then, remembering what I'd said earlier, I added the clincher. "Don't forget, he lets me do anything I want."

"That's right," Ellen said slowly.

"Now I'm *really* jealous," Jessica said, shaking her head. "My parents would never *dream* of letting me have a big party at our house. Mom says Unicorn meetings are bad enough."

"My mom says the same thing," Mandy said, rolling her eyes.

"Mine too," Ellen agreed. "So you guys had better pick up all that popcorn you spilled before she finds it."

"My mom goes ballistic if there's even *one crumb* of popcorn on the floor after a meeting," Kimberly said happily.

I frowned. Why did they all sound so proud? Here they were, complaining about their parents and the rules they put up with—and yet I felt as though they were boasting.

"Are you *sure* he won't mind, Lila?" Mandy asked softly.

I was sure. Well, ninety-nine percent sure anyway. I could see myself having a conversation with him at the dinner table. . . .

ME: Um, Dad?

DAD (smiling at me): What is it, sweetheart?

ME (smiling back): Dad, I'd like to have a party at the house on Saturday, and I was wondering—

DAD (heartily): And you wanted to know if that was all right? Why, of course it is, dear. I trust you.

ME (looking shyly down at my food): Thanks, Dad. I knew you'd understand.

DAD (nodding): You're so responsible and mature, sweetheart, that I couldn't possibly say no. . . .

It sounded good, all right. The only problem was, I could also imagine a conversation going like this:

ME: Dad?

DAD (hiding behind stock reports): What is it, Lila?

ME: Um, could I, you know, marry an ax murderer?

DAD (vaguely): I trust your judgment, Lila.

ME: Oh. Um, thanks. And while I'm at it, can I tear down the house and move into the Statue of Liberty?

DAD (tapping in a number on his cell phone): Sure. Nothing's too good for my little girl. . . .

"Lila?" Mandy pressed.

There was a lump in my throat. But I nodded anyway. "No problem," I said aloud, trying to smile brightly.

"Dad?" I asked at breakfast Friday morning.

Dad had the newspaper against his nose. "Yes, dear?" he asked, not bothering to look over at me.

I fiddled with my spoon. "Could we go to the mall today? You and me? After school? Together?"

I hadn't slept very well the night before. If the truth be told, my conscience was bothering me a little.

Well, OK. A lot.

Partly because of Jimmy. I still hadn't told Dad that Jimmy was so much older than me. If Dad knew about it, he just might want me to stop seeing Jimmy. Cancel our date that night and everything.

Second was the party. I wanted Dad to tell me the party was a great idea, that I was mature enough to carry it off. I was afraid he'd say, *You're just a kid! Forget about it.*

But mostly, I'd decided, I wanted him to know. To know about the party. And to know about Jimmy. If Dad was going to let me have the party and go out with an older guy, I wanted it to be because he thought I could handle it. Not because he couldn't be bothered to listen.

Slowly Dad lowered his newspaper. "I beg your pardon?"

I bit my lip. "Um—I thought maybe we could go to the mall this afternoon," I said. I would sort of work my way up to telling him about Jimmy and the party. And in the meantime we could spend some father-daughter time together. "Or if you don't like the mall," I added hastily, "there are other things. . . ."

Dad shook his head. "Sorry, sweetie," he said. "But I can't possibly. I have a golf date."

"Oh," I said, toying with my cereal. "Well, couldn't you cancel?"

"Oh, no!" Dad looked as if I'd asked him to rob a bank. "These guys have flown in from the Midwest, Lila. We've got to talk business."

I sighed and dropped my spoon into the bowl, where it slid slowly beneath the milk. Great. Business was always first. I should have known. "Can't you just this once?" I asked. "Please, Dad? I really need—"

Dad shook his head. "It's just not possible, dear."

I really need you, I finished sorrowfully in my head. Well, it clearly wasn't going to happen. There was a lump in my throat as big as a truck.

Dad folded his paper and stood up. "Of course, if there are things you need," he said, fumbling in his pocket, "then use these. Go buy yourself a treat. Take your mind off your troubles." He pressed something into my hand—something hard and plastic. He kissed the air above my head and headed for the driveway.

I narrowed my lips. I could tell by the feel that he'd given me credit cards. Credit cards! How could he think that credit cards would take my mind off my troubles?

I didn't want to go to the mall alone. I wanted to go with him. So that we could talk. I didn't need *things*—I needed *him!* A fury rose inside me. I threw the cards onto the table. Angrily I turned and ran toward the driveway myself.

I'd *make* him notice me. I'd *force* him to listen. I'd tell him the truth, the whole truth, and nothing but the truth, and see how he felt about that!

"I have a date tonight!" I called loudly as Dad got into his Lexus. My hands clenched and unclenched.

"That's nice," Dad said. He didn't even look at me. He reached for the door.

I took a deep breath. I was so angry now, I didn't care what I said. "He's older than me!" I shouted. "Like, lots older! He's in high school!"

There. I'd said it. I waited for Dad to answer.

But he didn't. The engine in the gold car leaped to life. Dad shifted into reverse and backed out of the driveway, pulling down the driver's-side visor so he wouldn't have to squint into the sun.

Or so he wouldn't have to see my face. I wasn't sure which.

My blood boiled.

And at the same time I felt like I would break down in tears any moment.

* * *

I had never felt so alone in my whole life. Slowly I walked back to the dining room. So business and a golf date were more important than me, Dad's only daughter. Or maybe I should call him "Fowler Enterprises" from now on. I could see myself introducing myself to strangers: *Hello there, I'm Lila Fowler, daughter of Fowler Enterprises.*

It was almost funny.

But it was too true for me to laugh.

On the table were the gold cards he'd given me. I shuddered. "So you think credit cards will win me over, huh, Dad?" I asked aloud.

I picked one up and ran my finger along its edge. I was about to cut it into a zillion pieces and send it back to the bank with a note that said, *Sorry, I am emotionally bankrupt. Sincerely, Mr. Fowler,* but then I paused.

What had Dad said? *Go buy yourself a treat*—that was it. I stared thoughtfully at the card in my hand.

I'd told Dad about Jimmy, and he hadn't listened. I hadn't told him about the party, but it was clear he wouldn't pay any attention to that either. So I'd done all I could.

I made my mouth a tight line.

Go buy myself a treat, huh, Dad? I thought. *Well, all right. If you insist!*

"You can't buy this one too," Jessica said, frowning.

Ellen nodded nervously. "You're already buying, what, three swimsuits?"

"Four," I said, slapping a credit card down on the counter. Four designer swimsuits, not all of them in my size, two of them so skimpy I wouldn't wear them in a private hot tub, and all of them costing a ton. "You can *never* have too many swimsuits."

"I know, but—" Jessica began. Then she must have seen the fire in my eyes, and she shrugged and turned away.

It was after school. I was making the rounds of the finest, fanciest stores in the entire mall, buying whatever appealed to me, plus a whole bunch of expensive things that didn't. Ellen and Jessica were along mostly to help me carry the bags.

"That will be five hundred thirty-four dollars and ninety-eight cents," the clerk informed me. "Will that be cash?"

I pointed to the credit card. Then I tapped my fingers impatiently on the countertop. If there's one thing I can't stand, it's dippy salesclerks.

"Of course, miss," she said, picking up the credit card and holding it between her fingertips as if it had head lice.

"But Lila," Ellen murmured, "are you *sure* your dad wanted you to buy all this stuff?"

"He gave me the credit cards, didn't he?" I demanded.

"Miss?" the clerk asked doubtfully. She held the credit card out to me, a worried look on her face. "I'm getting a warning here," she said, tapping the card machine in front of her.

"I knew it," Ellen said softly.

"According to the credit card company, too much money has been spent on this card today," the clerk went on. "The card hasn't reached its pre-set spending limit, of course, but there's a built-in warning that gets activated when spending is too high on any particular day."

"Then override it," I said.

"I beg your pardon?" The clerk stared at me in disbelief.

"Override it," I repeated. "Or perhaps you don't know whose card this is?"

The woman peered at the name imprinted on the card. "Oh, my!" she gulped. "Fowler. That wouldn't be—" She looked me over carefully. "Not *the* Fowler of Fowler Enterprises?"

"His daughter," I explained. "The card belongs to my father." It was all I could do not to add "Mr. Enterprises."

"Oh, in *that* case," the clerk said. "If you're *that* Fowler, then of course we'll just ignore the warning." She rang up the sale, wrapped the swimsuits, and handed the bag to me. "Have a nice day," she told me with a weak smile.

"Thank you," I said. "I'm sure I will." I tossed the bag onto Jessica's pile. I figured quickly in my head. I'd bought the swimsuits for more than five hundred dollars, and some exotic skin-care stuff for about three hundred, and then the sports gear . . . five plus three plus six, carry the one . . .

Well, a whole lot of money, that was for sure. But it was all for a good cause.

Me.

If I couldn't get my dad's attention any other way, I'd run up his bills until he noticed.

"Lovely," I said a few minutes later. "Just what I've always wanted. A hand-painted tea-leaf box."

Behind me, Jessica groaned.

"May I help you?" the clerk asked. He was a nice-looking young man in a fancy suit. But not as nice-looking as Jimmy.

"Yes, please," I said, slapping down my credit card.

"What about this one?" I asked my friends, pausing by a painting of a ship in a storm. It looked pretty ugly to me, but I wanted to know what Ellen and Jessica thought.

Jessica curled her lip. "Kind of stupid, if you ask me."

Ellen nodded. "My little brother could do better than that."

"Then I'll take it." I flipped my credit card onto the counter. "Charge it, please," I said in the most bored-sounding voice I could manage.

"Oh." The clerk's face changed expression. "Oh. I'm sorry, miss. I didn't realize that you were, um, *Mr. Fowler's* daughter." He rubbed his hands nervously. "Of course. We'll take care of that silly warning right away."

"See that you do," I said, folding my arms. The

shoes in front of me were kicky little things, and they almost even fit.

Who knows, I thought, *I might actually get around to wearing them one of these days.*

Sweating profusely, the clerk ran my card through again and rang the shoes up.

Too bad they're on sale, I thought.

"I didn't know you liked hard rock, Lila," Ellen said. We were at the front of the line at Totally Hip. She swung my overflowing basket of CDs from one hand to the other.

"Yeah," Jessica put in. "There's got to be close to a thousand bucks' worth of music in there. Are you positive—"

"Positive," I said with a wave of my hand. "And I'm not really a metalhead, Ellen. I'm just doing this for—"

I thought hard as I shoved the gold card at the clerk.

"For a friend," I finished with a little laugh.

"Oooh," Ellen sighed dreamily as we walked into the jewelry store. "Did you see those to-die-for unicorn pendants in the window?"

"Are they expensive?" I asked.

Ellen looked closely. "I can't find a price. But they're platinum."

I waved my hand dismissively. "Let's buy them," I told Ellen. "There are, what, five of us in the club? Let's get one for everybody. We'll wear them to the party."

Ellen's mouth opened as wide as a saucer. "Lila!"

"You don't know how much these cost," Jessica said, staring at the display. "The price tag doesn't show, and I bet they're not exactly cheap. In fact—"

I held up my hand to interrupt her and turned to Ellen. "Get them, would you?"

Nodding, Ellen scurried away and soon found a salesclerk to help her.

I flagged down the other clerk in the store. "Give me five of these necklaces, please," I demanded, pointing to a case filled with diamonds and pearls.

The clerk's jaw dropped. "Five?" she repeated.

"Five," I said testily. "Do I have to take my business someplace else?" I dropped the gold card on the counter.

The clerk looked at the card. Then she looked at me. "Um—of course not," she said, opening the lid of the case with a tiny key. "It's just that, well, the cheapest in here would be—"

"Money is no object," I said grandly.

But I was lying. Money *was* an object. Right then, money was the only object.

The clerk swallowed hard. "Very well. Now, this one here is lovely." She pointed to the smallest necklace of all.

I curled my upper lip. "I was looking for something a little more expensive," I said.

The clerk nodded. "Very good, miss."

"So nice to have a father who cares about you," I said aloud as the clerk rang up all the items, including the five unicorn pendants. "So nice to have a father who would give you the shirt off his back." But of course, he'd still have seventy more shirts hanging in the closet.

"Miss?" The clerk frowned.

I sighed. "Is there a problem?"

"I-I'm afraid so," the clerk stammered. "It seems that you have exceeded your limit on this card." She leaned forward. "Your credit limit is $75,000," she said, adjusting her glasses, "and the purchase of five necklaces and five pendants would take you over that limit."

"Seventy-five *thousand?*" Ellen hissed.

"No problem," I said stonily. And I whipped out another one of the cards Dad had given me.

I really, truly didn't care how much money I was spending.

The idea was wonderful and horrifying at the same time.

But as long as my dad wouldn't listen when I tried to talk to him, what other choice did I have?

Nine

Jimmy sat up straighter in his chair and grinned at me sheepishly. He adjusted his sport coat, which didn't quite fit. I guessed he'd borrowed it from his dad. "So," he said.

I nodded. "So?" I asked with a smile.

Jimmy took a deep breath. "So, um, what do you want to talk about?"

Jimmy and I were at the exact same table I'd had on Sunday night. It was a little more crowded now, though, since it was Friday. I'd been hoping that Caroline Pearce would be there too, so Lila-and-Jimmy would replace Lila-sitting-alone as the gossip item of the day, but I guess most people don't make two trips to Chez François in one week.

Except for Fowlers.

I smiled again. "Oh, I don't know," I said. "What

do you want to talk about?" What I wanted, of course, was for him to look into my eyes dreamily and say, *Here's to the most beautiful girl at Sweet Valley Middle School.* But I couldn't think of a good way of getting into a conversation like that.

Jimmy licked his lips a little nervously. "Um—well—" He shrugged. "The food's pretty decent."

I looked down at what was left of my Cornish game hen with cilantro. I suspected François wouldn't be happy to hear his food called "pretty decent." "One of those restaurant review books gives it five stars," I told him.

"Five stars?" Jimmy raised his eyebrows. "Is that good?"

I tried not to laugh. It was obvious Jimmy wasn't used to the finer things in life. "Five stars is the best," I told him. "There are maybe ten restaurants in the whole United States that get rated that high."

Jimmy looked down at his plate. "So this is, like, one of the ten best restaurants in the country?" he asked. "How about the Dairi Burger? Doesn't that crack the list?"

I sighed. "I don't think they rate places like the Dairi Burger, Jimmy."

Jimmy shifted uncomfortably in his chair. "I was teasing."

"Oh." I felt a little embarrassed.

"Anyway, I do like this food," Jimmy went on, flashing that incredible grin. I'd seen it a dozen times now, and I still swooned every time. "Be sure to thank your dad for me."

My dad? I frowned. *Oh, right, my dad!* He was the one who'd let me invite a friend to Chez François. At least that was what I'd told Jimmy. "I will," I promised. But I couldn't look him in the eye, and there was a knot in the pit of my stomach.

As if by magic, a waiter appeared and took my plate.

"They'll be back in a minute with the dessert cart," I told Jimmy. "They make fabulous chocolate mousse. They also do this awesome *café brûlot framboise,* and if we're lucky, they'll have *coeur à la crème.*" I could feel my mouth begin to water.

Jimmy bit his lip. *"Coeur à la* who?"

"Coeur à la crème," I said. "It's like cheesecake."

"Oh!" A slow smile spread across Jimmy's face. "Cheesecake. I like cheesecake. What's that other stuff you mentioned?"

"Café brûlot framboise?" I said. "It's so cool! It's, like, this rich, sweet flaming coffee—"

Jimmy winced. "I think I'll stick with the cheesecake, thanks," he said.

I fell silent. I felt a little bad for Jimmy. But he hadn't grown up on French food, so I couldn't expect him to like these things first time out.

Well, if I have anything to say about it, I thought, *you'll be coming back again, Jimmy!* Maybe we could make it a Friday night tradition.

"So," Jimmy said again, and he adjusted his sport

coat once more. "This is, you know, pretty cool."

It'll be even more cool in a minute, I thought. I reached below the table, pulled out a brightly wrapped package, and held it out to him.

"What's this?" Jimmy asked curiously.

"A little something for you," I said. "Open it!"

Jimmy yanked off the wrapping paper. Reaching into the box, he pulled out the deluxe diving watch I'd bought for him at the sporting goods store earlier in the afternoon. Frowning, he stared from the watch to my face and back.

I swallowed hard. "Don't you like it?" I asked, but the words seemed to catch in my throat.

Jimmy wiggled the watch this way and that, examining it intently. "I *love* it!" he exclaimed. "This is so awesome, Lila! How did you know I've always wanted one of these things?"

"Oh, just a lucky guess," I said.

Which was the absolute truth.

Jimmy grinned. Without a word of warning, he leaned over the table and gave me a kiss on the cheek.

I swear my heart stopped beating. I could hardly breathe. Every inch of my skin seemed to tingle. *If only Caroline Pearce had seen that!* I thought. It was all I could do not to faint away into Jimmy's arms.

"This is so incredibly cool," Jimmy went on. He'd settled back into his chair and was turning the watch over and over in his hands, but I scarcely noticed. I decided I'd never wash that cheek again. At least not until Jimmy's next kiss. Which, I hoped, wouldn't be too much longer. Gently I rubbed the spot with my fingertips. It felt different, that was for sure. Still warm from the pressure of his lips and—

"Lila?"

With a start I looked up. Jimmy was holding the watch out to me. "I—I really can't accept this, you know," he said softly, and he lowered his eyes. "It's way too expensive. I mean, I couldn't afford this in a million years."

My blood ran cold. I'd never dreamed that Jimmy wouldn't accept it. "Oh, but you *have* to!" I protested. "It didn't cost as much as you think—" No, that made it sound like it was fake. Or used. "I mean, I won't take it back." Dramatically I folded my hands into my lap.

Jimmy sighed. "But Lila, after this dinner and all—"

"I won't take no for an answer," I told him.

Jimmy scratched his head. Then he grinned his awesome grin. "OK," he said. "If you're sure." His eyes sparkled, and he gently slid the watch out of its holder and around his wrist.

Slowly I exhaled. I hadn't realized I'd been holding my breath. "It looks really cool on you," I said sincerely.

Jimmy nodded. "Yeah," he said. "Hey, thanks. I mean it."

I looked down at the table, smiling to myself. It felt really good to be able to shower Jimmy with presents.

"This is *so* cool," Jimmy said. He flexed his arm,

admiring the watch from every angle. "Now all I need is a powerboat to dive from, and, hey! I'm all set!" He laughed.

A powerboat, I thought. *Check!*

Mentally I wrote it down.

"The beach is really beautiful this time of night, isn't it?" I asked Jimmy a little later.

Dinner was over, and we'd taken off our shoes and socks to walk along the sand. The moonlight streamed across the calm waters of the ocean, and in the distance I saw the lights of a pier. The sand felt smooth against my toes. "Isn't it?" I repeated, turning to look at Jimmy.

He smiled down at me, the corners of his mouth crinkling in a way that made my heart want to stop beating. "It sure is," he said.

"Um—Jimmy?" I asked. "Some of us—I mean, my friends and me—" *Aren't you supposed to say 'my friends and I'?* I wondered. "Um—my friends and I—tomorrow night—" I took a deep breath. This wasn't coming out right. "I belong to this club, and we're having a party at my house tomorrow," I said quickly. "I sure hope you can come. It wouldn't be the same without you."

I looked up at him anxiously, afraid he'd say no.

Jimmy stopped and turned to face me. His bare foot kicked a clump of sand lying on the beach, and the grains scattered in all directions. He smiled easily. "Tomorrow?"

I nodded. "I don't think you've been to my house, but it's pretty neat," I said. "There's a pool and a ballroom, and we'll have the place decorated like you wouldn't believe, and we're looking into bands, and—" I ran out of air.

Jimmy took my hand in his. "Could I bring along some of my friends?" he asked.

My heart soared. If Jimmy wanted me to meet his friends, that meant he really liked me, didn't it? It made going out together official.

Of course, that guy Newcombe's kind of a jerk, I thought, remembering the way he'd acted at Casey's. But I was sure some of Jimmy's teammates were fun. And having a few high-school kids around wouldn't be a problem. If anything, it would spread the Unicorn Club's name a little further. Mandy would be proud. "Sure," I said, feeling the warmth of his hand in mine.

Jimmy smiled warmly. "Then I'd love to."

"Great," I said, almost giddy with delight.

Dad would have a conniption if he knew I was having a bunch of high-school boys over to the house without any adults around. At least I thought he would.

Lila the rebel. The name sounded great.

Well, if Dad wasn't going to pay attention to me, then he deserved whatever he got.

I tightened my grip on Jimmy's fingers. "Hey, bring the whole high school if you want!" I told him.

Ten

What my family means to me.

I sighed and read the essay topic one more time, hoping it would turn into something else. It was late Friday night, and I was trying to get my homework out of the way—believe it or not!—so I could concentrate on the party the next day. *What My Family Means to Me,* I wrote at the top of the page, centering it neatly.

Well, let's see. I have a dad who's never home and never pays attention to me when he is home, like now, and a mom who ran off the first time she saw me, and—

Jessica wouldn't have any trouble with this assignment, I thought. Neither would Mandy. They'd complain and moan about it, but at least they would have something to write about. I sighed. My conscience was bothering me again about Jimmy and about the party. But if Dad wouldn't listen, what could I do?

Maybe I'd fax him at work or something. I added the date to the paper and looked at the blank lines stretching endlessly in front of me.

The phone rang.

I eyed the receiver longingly. It was probably Ellen or Jessica or somebody calling about the party. I bit my lip. "I sort of have to do my homework," I told it.

Two rings. Three.

Well, maybe I could get excused from doing the assignment because I don't really have a family. Quickly I grabbed the receiver before the machine picked up. "Hello?"

"Hi, Lila."

It was a guy's voice. For a fraction of a second I didn't know whose. But my heart started beating furiously, and then my brain figured it out. "Jimmy?" I half whispered.

"Yeah, it's me." Jimmy sounded grown-up and confident. "I just wanted to thank you again for the watch. And for the wonderful evening." He laughed that little laugh I loved so much. "It isn't every day I get to eat at a place like Chez François."

I was about to reply, *Really? I do,* but I caught myself in time. "Well, I'm glad we had the chance," I said, hoping I sounded sophisticated.

Jimmy laughed again. "Will you thank your dad for me too?"

Suddenly I had a brainstorm. Dad was in his study next door, getting ready to leave later that night on a business trip. If I put Jimmy on the line with him, even Dad would realize that Jimmy was lots older than me. He'd have to. And then we could have a real, frank, heart-to-heart talk about boyfriends, and dating, and parties, and—

And maybe I'd have something to write about for my essay after all.

"Hang on a moment, Jimmy," I blurted out. "Let me put him on the line for you." I put my cordless phone on mute and headed over to my dad's study.

"Dad?" I called, bursting through the door. He was sitting at his burnished oak desk, clicking away at the keyboard of his computer. The display on the screen showed a spreadsheet crammed full of numbers. "Dad?"

Dad didn't turn around. "Just a minute, sweetie," he said.

I couldn't wait. "Dad?" I said. "This is really important. My boyfriend is on the phone." I waited for a reaction from Dad, but there wasn't one. The keyboard kept clicking.

Nervously I licked my lips, but I didn't give up. "My *older* boyfriend," I said loudly, pronouncing every word as carefully as I could, "who is in *high* school, is on the phone, and he wants to thank you for the incredibly *expensive* dinner you treated us to earlier tonight."

There. I'd said it.

Dad clicked a few more keys. The display vanished, and another spreadsheet took its place. "That's nice."

I stared in astonishment at my father. Jessica's

father would have gone ballistic. So would Mandy's. So would any *real* father. "Didn't you hear me?" I asked, feeling my chest constrict. "My high-school boyfriend's on the phone, and he wants to thank you personally."

Dad peered at the screen. "No problem," he said absently. "Tell him I said hello."

I stared at my father, anger rising in my throat. I wanted to scream and yell and throw something through the screen of his precious computer. But I didn't. I was a big girl now. I whirled around and stalked back into my room, settling for slamming the door behind me.

Dad hadn't heard a word I'd said! Not one single solitary word!

And it had to be because he didn't care. Because he really, truly, did not care about me.

"Jimmy?" I said as calmly as I could into the phone. "He's busy, but he says you're very welcome."

I sounded calm, but inside I was seething. I'd made up my mind. No way was I telling Dad about the party now. No way was I telling him about Jimmy. Dad could go rot.

"Well, thanks for passing the message on anyway," Jimmy said. "Your dad must be a great guy, Lila. I hope I'll get to meet him someday."

I grinned my killer grin. "Maybe you will, Jimmy," I promised.

But not anytime soon!

*   *   *

"You're sure you can do it?" I asked Jessica nervously.

"No problem," Jessica assured me. "Give me that phone!"

It was Saturday morning, and I was at the Wakefields'. My father had already left for his business trip, but we'd suddenly remembered that Mrs. Pervis was still around. That was no good, because she'd throw a fit when the van filled with cases of soda pulled up. Luckily, Jessica had a plan to get rid of her.

Oh, not permanently, of course.

Jessica put the receiver to her ear. "I wish you could remember the name of your dad's secretary," she hissed as she dialed. "It would make it a lot easier—oh, hello, is this Mrs. Pervis?"

I leaned across Jessica's bed and closer to the phone, but I couldn't hear much.

"Hi, Mrs. P.," Jessica said breezily. "This is me, Mr. Fowler's secretary." She listened for a moment and then went on. "That's right, Mrs. Grassi."

I wrinkled my nose. *Mrs. Grassi! Of course!*

"What?" Jessica listened again. "Oh, that's because I have a slight cold today, Mrs. P." She coughed loudly and cleared her throat. "I've been inhaling aspirin today, you just don't *know*. Anyway, there's been a change in plan. Mr. F. was suddenly called to Greece, and he'd like Lila to join him for the rest of the weekend."

Jessica listened some more. I leaned even closer, trying to find out what was going on. My heart was beating fast.

"I agree, Mrs. P.," Jessica said, rolling her eyes. "It *is* a little strange for him to want Lila—I know they're not big on family time—"

I looked down at Jessica's bedspread.

"Where in Greece?" Jessica looked frantically at me. "Um—hang on a moment, Mrs. P., I've got it right here. . . ."

I strained to think of cities in Greece. "Rome?" I mouthed.

"Rome!" Jessica announced triumphantly. She pressed the phone closer to her ear. "Oh, is that right? Dear me, I must have the wrong sheet of paper." She covered the mouthpiece. "Rome's in *Italy*, doofus!" she snarled at me.

"Oops." I smiled weakly.

"Well, I think Mr. F.'s come down with a serious case of midlife crisis," Jessica said into the receiver. "When men hit a certain age, they like to be surrounded by their near and dear." Quickly she plowed ahead. "But the point is, Mrs. P., you can go visit your daughter in Sunshine Falls!"

Jessica grinned across at me and gave me a thumbs-up sign. Then, just as quickly, the grin faded.

"Oh," she said slowly. "Um—did I *say* I was Mrs. Grassi?" She bit her lip. "Of course not—I know that Mrs. Grassi would never, ever call you 'Mrs. P.'" She blushed and fidgeted with the cord, staring daggers in my direction. "I'm not Mrs. Grassi at all," Jessica went on. "I just said that to make things a little simpler, ha ha. I'm really, um—" Jessica took a deep breath. "I'm really Mrs. Grassi's secretary."

The secretary's secretary? I stared at Jessica in horror. "She'll never believe that," I whispered frantically.

But a grin was beginning to grow on Jessica's face. "Well, nice to talk to you too," she said. "So you can leave this morning for Sunshine Falls, the earlier the better."

There was a pause. I clutched Jessica's shoulder. I could feel my heart hammering. The earlier the better?

Jessica laughed nervously. "Of course we're not trying to get rid of you, Mrs. P.! But I know you wouldn't want to miss a minute of precious time with your daughter." Quickly she said good-bye and hung up.

"Well?" I asked, afraid to hear the answer.

"Relax." Jessica flashed me a brilliant smile. "She bought it!"

"I can come in with you, miss," Richard said through the intercom. "Won't take but a moment."

He guided the limo expertly through the heavy traffic at the airport. We were on the small access road that led to the departure gates.

I took a deep breath. This hadn't been part of the plan. Jessica and I had gotten rid of Mrs. Pervis—but I hadn't realized she would insist that Richard drive me to the airport.

It's kind of strange, riding in a limo to catch a

nonexistent plane. Especially when you don't have a ticket for it to begin with.

"Oh, no, please!" I said quickly. Too quickly. I gave a little laugh. "I'm sorry, Richard," I explained. "I just want to do it myself now. Now that I'm, you know, older."

"Very good, miss," Richard said, swinging the wheel sharply to the right.

I pressed my nose to the window. The airport was busy, all right. It had taken us too long to get there, and I was worried about getting back in time for the start of the party. I'd really hoped to show Jimmy off—

The limo jerked to a stop.

I clutched my flight bag, stuffed to the brim with eight sweaters. "Bye, Richard!" I called, pushing the door handle open. "Remember, you have all weekend off. See you on Monday." I swung my feet out of the limo.

Screech! A car skidded by, missing my knees by two inches. I screamed. The intercom crackled. "Miss Lila!" Richard cried. "You're exiting on the wrong side of the vehicle!"

I scrambled back in and slammed the door. My heart was threatening to pop out of my chest. "Oh, right," I said with as much dignity as I could manage. "I knew that." Then I climbed out the proper side. Brushing the sweat off my brow, I stood on the sidewalk, waving, until Richard disappeared.

I'd made it to the airport. Now all I needed was to get back. I looked for a cab. *Let's see—do I have enough money?* I groped in my pocket. All I had was traveler's checks, which Mrs. Pervis had given me just before she left town. Traveler's checks were a pain in the neck, but they'd do, I decided.

Cabdrivers took traveler's checks, right?

"Taxi!" I yelled, stepping confidently into the roadway.

Eleven

I thrust three twenty-dollar bills into the cabdriver's hand. "Keep the change," I told him. Quickly I slammed the door and headed up the driveway.

Forty-five minutes late to my own party!

How come nobody had *told* me that cabdrivers don't take traveler's checks or credit cards? I'd had to buy some stuff at the gift shop to cash one of the traveler's checks, and *of course* Mrs. Pervis had gotten me hundred-dollar denominations, and—

I stopped and stared. I'd never seen so many people in my life.

The house and grounds were crawling with kids. The pool was so full, I didn't think another body would fit in it. There were people laughing, talking, eating, and chasing each other all over the lawn, and there were even a few kids climbing onto the roof.

Through my bedroom window!

I dropped the flight bag and broke into a run. I didn't even recognize half the kids. My stomach churned. This wasn't what I'd had in mind at all.

If this was a Unicorn party, then where were the Unicorns?

A tall blond boy intercepted me as I approached the house. Newcombe! I froze.

"You're kind of late," he said accusingly, spitting a mouthful of ginger ale all over the walk.

All over my dad's prized flagstones! My stomach churned harder. "Well, the cab was late," I said weakly.

"Oh, don't bother about *her*, Newcombe," said someone behind me. "Just another middle-school dweeb, that's all."

"Uh-huh," Newcombe said with a sneer. He turned away from me. "Don't know why they're letting middle-school kids in, do you?"

"Because I happen to live here!" I snarled furiously. "This is my house, you jerk!"

Newcombe frowned at me. "Yeah, right," he said, and his lips curved into a mocking grin. He turned back to his friends. "She owns the place!" he said in a singsong voice.

"Oooh!" somebody squeaked.

I bit back an answer and walked by quickly. The truth was, Newcombe and his friends scared me just a little.

"Cowabunga!" The voice echoed from the swimming pool. A stack of people three high rose out of the water. At the top was a high-school girl in an incredibly skimpy bikini—skimpier than the designer suits I'd bought earlier that week. The kid at the bottom lurched while the girl at the top shrieked and tried to keep her balance. It looked incredibly dangerous.

Another pile of kids appeared, bobbing and weaving. I gasped. They were playing chicken! I was sure that any minute one of the piles would topple over. Someone would hit their head on the side of the pool and—

Can you say lawsuit? I thought grimly.

"Gotcha!" The girl grabbed the boy at the top of the other pile and shoved hard. With a screech, he tumbled backward—straight for the diving board!

I couldn't stand to look. But of course I did anyway. The boy somersaulted down, barely missing the board, and landed on top of a couple of kids who were eating cookies in the pool. Water and cookies flew everywhere.

The kid who'd fallen came up for air. "What a dive!" he boasted. "Olympics, here I come!"

I took a deep breath. *He doesn't have a clue how close he came to causing a serious accident,* I thought angrily. Half-eaten cookies were floating around the pool. The tower of kids that was still standing was wiggling back and forth so violently that I thought the girl on top would tumble down next. I wanted to yell at the kids, but there were too many of them.

And they were too big.

Suddenly I felt very small and very young.

"Look out beloooooow!" Startled, I glanced up—
and gasped. The kids on the roof were pushing a
big guy in blue jeans over the edge. I watched, my
heart in my mouth, as he tucked his body into a
cannonball and splashed into the center of the pool,
just missing a boy in cutoffs lying on a raft.

"Awesome!" somebody shouted. "My turn next!"

I felt faint. Two inches to the right and—

"Lila!" Ellen ran up, breathing heavily. "Thank
goodness you're here!"

It was oddly comforting to see a familiar face. I
opened my mouth to speak, but Ellen kept going.
"Things have been out of control since the beginning of the party!" she said. "There were, like, six
carloads of high-school kids when we opened up,
and it's just gotten worse ever since! Jessica tried to
talk to them, but they ignored her."

I bit my lip. If they ignored Jessica, things were
pretty bleak.

"They trashed the tables we set up," Ellen was
saying, "and the drinks ran out fifteen minutes
ago, and they rolled one of your dad's planters
into the pool, and it's amazing that no one's been
seriously hurt, and more high-school kids have
been arriving ever since, and where are they coming from anyway?"

But I was barely listening. "Where's Jimmy?" I
demanded, grabbing Ellen's sleeve. They'd listen to
Jimmy, I knew it. I remembered how he'd told off
Newcombe at Casey's. Jimmy could fix this. If—

If he wasn't one of the kids who was causing the damage. My stomach ached.

"Jimmy?" Ellen looked blank. "Huh?"

I felt a surge of annoyance. "Never mind," I told Ellen. "I'll take care of it."

I dashed behind the house, scanning faces. Once in a while I recognized a middle-school kid, Bruce Patman or Maria Slater or somebody. But they were all standing off to the side, and anyway there were way more high-school kids. I felt a twinge of guilt. This party was supposed to impress the other kids our age, not terrify them. "Jimmy?" I called, trying to make myself heard over the constant noise.

"You mean Jimmy Lancer?" Evie Kim poked her head out from the side of the house, where she was huddled with Elizabeth Wakefield and Mary Wallace. "He's in there." She nodded toward the door of the living room.

"Thanks," I said breathlessly. Through the doorway I could see Jimmy's back. I ran through piles of soda cans and streamers that someone had pulled down. "Jimmy!" I cried.

It will be all right, I told myself. *Jimmy will tell them to leave. Then the middle-school kids will have a good time and everyone will see how close Jimmy and I have become.*

I skidded to a stop. "Hi, Jimmy," I said, pasting my best smile on my face and leaning my elbow comfortably on his shoulder. It was amazing, the effect he had on me. Already I felt calmer, and I was sure my heart had stopped racing.

Jimmy turned. "Oh, hi, Lila!" he said, flashing me that amazing smile. He thrust his arm quickly around my waist. "Great party, kid!"

Kid? I frowned. "Um—thanks," I said. "Listen, I really need your help—"

"Jimmy!" To my surprise, a pair of arms suddenly wrapped themselves around Jimmy's shoulders from the back. A pair of arms that obviously belonged to a girl.

I gasped. My heart gave a lurch. When Jimmy had asked to bring along friends, I thought he'd meant—you know—boys. "Um—Jimmy?" I croaked out, not wanting to believe my eyes.

"Hey, Hilary!" Jimmy leaned back and puckered his lips. "Been looking all over for you, sweetie."

Hilary Smithwick giggled and craned her neck around his, not noticing me. They kissed lightly, and Jimmy pulled Hilary to his side. My mouth went absolutely dry. I stared. I willed my eyes to close, but I couldn't tear them away.

"And I've been looking for you!" Hilary said with a grin.

I couldn't say a word. I couldn't even breathe. I just stood there, swaying back and forth, my mouth hanging wide open like a dork. Like the total loser I obviously was.

Jimmy and Hilary—kissing! At *my* party! And he didn't even have the decency to be embarrassed about it. I kept on staring, wishing the earth would open and swallow me up.

Jimmy seemed to notice me again. "Oh, Hilary," he said, waving his hand at me, "this is Lila. You know, the one I've been telling you about?"

"Lila!" Hilary said happily. "I've just been dying to meet you! Jimmy speaks so highly of you and everything!"

Huh? The blood drained from my face. What was Jimmy doing talking to Hilary about me anyway?

Hilary pressed up against Jimmy's chest and grinned. Jimmy smiled back and held her closer. "He just loves having a new little sister!" Hilary said, leaning against Jimmy's shoulder.

A new little sister. My hands clenched and unclenched. So Jimmy had never loved me at all.

"Yeah," Jimmy agreed, nuzzling the top of Hilary's head. "I've always wanted a little sister, you know. Meeting you was one of the best things that ever happened to me, Lila." He gave Hilary a wink. "Next to meeting Hilary, of course!"

The dinner. The Mangy Muttheads CD. The new diving watch. I couldn't believe how much money and time I'd spent trying to buy Jimmy's love. And it hadn't worked. Of course it hadn't worked. I looked down at the ground. Jimmy had never been interested, would never be interested. I was just a dumb little seventh-grader, and he was—

"Great party, Lila," Jimmy said.

"Yeah, totally awesome," Hilary echoed him.

But I couldn't take it any longer.

Bursting into tears, I turned and ran.

Twelve

"Lila?"

I ignored the voice and sobbed even harder. I was curled up behind a bush somewhere in the garden, crying my eyes out. I didn't care how long I'd been there. I didn't care who heard me. I didn't care what anybody thought. Jimmy didn't love me, and that was all that mattered.

"Lila!" There was a gentle push on my shoulder. Reluctantly I opened my eyes. Elizabeth Wakefield was standing over me, with Jessica close behind her.

"We've been looking all over for you," Elizabeth said. She bent down and squeezed my hand. "Evie saw you when you, ah, ran away from Jimmy, and—"

Tears stung my eyes. Jimmy. I knew I should be grateful to have friends who really cared about me, but at the moment I could only think about Jimmy. My heart was broken.

"C'mon." Elizabeth reached behind my back and pulled me to a sitting position. I went limp, but I didn't resist. "Tell us what happened."

"I—can't." My voice sounded like someone else's, and I was sure I looked ridiculous. My lower lip began to tremble. "I just can't."

"OK." Jessica reached for my hand. She squatted next to me on the ground, just being there for me.

Elizabeth reached in her pocket and pulled out a package of tissues. "Here," she said, offering me a handful. "You look like maybe you could use these."

I took them and blew my nose. Then I started to cry all over again. I felt worse than I had ever felt in my entire life. Jimmy was in love with somebody else, and I had been a total fool. How could I have been so wrong? So stupid?

I was on my fifth tissue when suddenly there was a loud screeching sound from the house. The noise of amplified guitars poured from an upstairs window.

"Huh?" The tissue fell from my hand.

Jessica wrinkled her nose. "Oh, the Mangy Muttheads," she said with a sigh. "Not one of my favorite groups."

The Mangy Muttheads! My mind flashed back to Totally Hip, when I'd bought Jimmy that CD. Twenty-five bucks down the toilet. Not to mention the watch, the other CDs, and all the other stuff I'd bought just to get Dad back.

Here I'd thought I was so incredibly cool. Lila on the loose. And I was just a stupid little kid trying to buy a life with plastic.

Suddenly I knew that this party had to end. I didn't want anybody around while I was upset, except my very closest friends. I certainly didn't want high-school kids playing on the roof, eating cookies in the pool, and turning the lawn into a trash dump.

I stood up and clenched my fists.

"Where are you going?" Jessica asked with surprise.

"To close down the party," I said. I wasn't sure how, but I was determined to try.

Not even caring that I probably looked like a total mess, I ran toward the pool.

"The party's over!" I yelled. My throat was sore. I didn't know how much longer I could keep this up.

Especially since no one was paying attention to me.

In the pool, kids splashed each other. I waved my hands frantically. "The party is *over!*" I shouted, jerking my thumb like a baseball umpire. "Everybody out of the pool, *now!*" I grabbed a stray elbow. "It's time to go home!"

The kid who owned the elbow glared at me. "What are you talking about?" he demanded.

"I said, the party is over!" I yelled.

The kid splashed me right in the face. "Yeah, right," he said. "Get a load of this kid," he laughed to a girl next to him. "She says the party's over!"

The girl snickered."Hey, this party's just *beginning!*" she said.

"Of course, your parents might not let *you* stay out late," the boy told me. "So *you* can clear out, but as for *us,* we're staying here." He turned to the girl and dunked her under the water.

"This is *my* house," I started to say, but then I shut my mouth. It was obvious that no one was listening. Maybe the pool wasn't the best place to start. I ran toward a group of kids sprawled across the lawn. "The party is over!" I yelled. They were all girls; maybe they'd hear me. "It's done, finished, history!"

The girls turned toward me. One sighed. "Go away," she muttered, adjusting her bikini top.

"Are you deaf?" I snapped. "The party's *over.* Clear out right now."

"Can it, kid." Another girl sat up. "This place is awesome. We'll be here for hours. Did you see the upstairs?"

The upstairs? I thought in a rage. *You mean* my *upstairs?* I choked back a reply. The Mangy Muttheads kept on blaring. One so-called song ended, and another began.

I wished I'd never gotten out of bed that morning. I wished I'd never agreed to have the party at my house. I wished I'd never *heard* of Jimmy Lancer. I wished—I wished—I wished—

Splat! A chunk of sod whizzed through the air and slammed against my shoulder.

"Hey, Newcombe! Nice shot!" called a voice I didn't recognize. I turned to see Newcombe bend down, pull another clump of soil and grass out of the ground, and let it fly. Dad's beautiful lawn!

Another kid pulled up an even larger handful of grass and dirt. "Bombs away!" he cried, throwing it high into the air. Little pieces of dirt flaked off and landed all over the place.

I clenched my fists. We would never be able to clean up all this mess. If they didn't leave that instant—

Someone jacked up the volume on the CD player.

Elizabeth appeared next to me. "Maybe we could blast a recording of our own," she suggested. "'Warning! The party is over! Leave now!' Something like that."

I didn't bother to answer. It would never work. I stared into the gathering darkness . . . and saw a pair of headlights cutting through the twilight. A car door slammed. Expecting more high-school students, I groaned—and then drew in my breath.

My father's gold Lexus was in the driveway, and my father himself was walking quickly up the flagstones.

"Dad!" I shouted, sprinting straight for him. I couldn't begin to decide if I was glad to see him or not. "Dad! What are you doing home?"

Dad stared at the house, mouth wide open in astonishment. "My trip was cut short," he said. "I have to leave for Hong Kong by midnight. Where's Mrs. Pervis?"

My mouth felt dry. "Gone, I guess. Oh, Dad, I'm so glad you're here! I'm so upset." I reached for him. I needed a fatherly hug in the worst way.

But Dad didn't seem to hear. Setting down his briefcase, he marched past me and over to the pool, where he grabbed a scruffy-looking kid by the neck.

"Hey, man!" The kid whirled around.

"Out," Dad said between clenched teeth, dragging the kid onto the pool's edge. "Out, all of you," he said. "Beat it!"

"Hey, man, don't have a cow!" The kid stood up and took a couple of steps backward.

My father pointed an accusing forefinger at him. "Do you understand English?" he demanded.

"OK, OK!" The kid stretched out his hands. "I'm history."

Suddenly the kids in the pool were completely silent. The only noise came from the Mangy Muttheads pulsing through the window. Dad had center stage, that was clear. I wished he'd come back and comfort me. *I need you, Dad,* I thought, biting my lip to keep back the tears.

"I'm going into the house to check for damage," Dad announced. "By the time I come out . . ." He stared ominously at all the kids. "Everyone had better be gone. And I mean *gone.*"

In twos and threes the kids started to pack up and drift off. One of the boys even fished the planter out of the pool before following his buddies down the driveway. Within seconds, the Mangy Muttheads went off in midsqueal.

I stared at the French doors that my father had stepped through. He'd gone inside and left me alone—just when I needed him most.

What about me, Dad? I asked myself silently, trying not to cry for what seemed like the thirteenth time that day.

It was clear that all Dad cared about was his dumb property—his house, his yard, his pool. There I was, practically in tears, and he didn't even notice. He didn't even care.

He could have asked, *What's wrong, honey?* He could have said, *Poor Lila! Tell me what happened to you!* But no.

I dug my foot into a hole in the ground and pushed my hand over my mouth so I wouldn't break down. "I'm going into the house to check for damage." Those were his exact words.

"Well, what about the damage to your daughter?" I screamed after him, knowing he couldn't possibly hear me.

And then, despite my best efforts, the tears started to flow again, and this time they seemed to well up from deeper than before. Through my tears I realized that I wasn't crying over some stupid crush. That was all I'd had with Jimmy, I realized now. No. These tears were about something much more serious.

I was crying for my father. My father, who was never there for me. My father, who ignored me when I needed him. My father, who—

The doors to the patio opened and he stepped out, a scowl on his face. Before I could think about what I was doing, I ran forward. "Forget the house!" I cried, my body shaking with sobs so strong I could barely get the words out. "You can always get another stupid house! But you can never get another daughter!"

There. I'd said it.

Dad sighed in a patronizing kind of way. "I'll get to you in due time, Lila," he said. His eyes flashed. "For starters, you're grounded. For a month, maybe two."

"You can't ground me!" I shot back. "You're leaving, and you won't be home again for who knows how long, and when you *are* home you don't notice what I do or who I do it with! So you can't ground me. It won't work!" I stared at Dad, eyes blazing.

"Lila—" Dad said warningly.

But I was too far gone to stop. "And a lot you care anyway!" I shouted. "You'll be off in Hong Kong making six gazillion *more* dollars! Well, who needs it?"

Dad rolled his eyes. "I'd love to stay and talk," he said, checking his watch, "but my flight leaves in only—"

Flights! Money! I was sick of it. "You think

money equals love!" I screamed in a voice that probably could have been heard on Mars. I knew now that money didn't equal love. Money hadn't bought me Jimmy's love, had it? "Well, all I have to say to you is this. You're not a father at all!" I dug deep for the worst insult I could think of. "You're an automatic teller machine!"

"Lila!" Dad's voice was firm. "Stop it this instant!"

But something inside me had snapped. I'd said my piece, and now I was miserable, more miserable than I had ever been in my entire life. I didn't care what Dad would do, I didn't care what he would say. I had to get out of there.

I turned and ran.

"Lila!" Dad's voice boomed behind me.

I didn't listen. Sobbing as if my heart would truly break, I headed through the darkness toward the old tree that was my secret hiding place. I shinnied up to the crook formed by the first branch.

I needed to be alone. And my dad would never find me there. Not that he would look, anyhow.

I hoped he stayed in Hong Kong for a week. A month. A year. A century.

I settled myself in the tree branches and sobbed.

I didn't care if I never saw my father again in my entire life.

Thirteen

My father was swimming in the ocean, in the middle of a thunderstorm. He was wearing an enormous deep-sea-diving suit, with Jimmy Lancer's new diving watch around his wrist. Huge waves crashed around his head and shoulders. I watched from the beach, completely furious with him.

"Dad!" I shouted, cupping my hands against the wind and rain. "Come out of that ocean right now!"

The only answer was a sizzling stroke of lightning that plunged into the water. Almost instantly there was a thunderclap so loud I had to cover my ears.

"Dad!" I yelled. I stamped my foot. Why didn't he pay attention?

Out in the ocean, Dad dived through a wave. Whitecaps rolled above his body. Surfacing, he kicked his legs frantically and looked around.

I wanted to do something to rescue him. But I didn't know how. I couldn't even move.

Dad opened his mouth and yelled. I leaned closer, trying to hear what he was saying. But the wind carried his words away.

"Dad!" I pleaded.

For a second the wind died down. Dad's mouth opened again. "Lila, where are you?" he called feebly, just before a wall of water hit his back.

I stood, stunned. Dad was looking for me!

"I'm here, Dad!" I shouted. My feet sprang to life. I hustled through the rain to the edge of the beach and dived. The ocean enveloped me like a warm coat.

"Lila!" my dad called weakly. . . .

"Lila! Lila!" But suddenly the voice was in my ear. My eyes jerked open. I felt terribly uncomfortable. The beach was nowhere in sight, and I realized that I was wedged into the crook of my tree. And I was soaking wet—soaking with rainwater.

It was all only a dream.

"Lila." A familiar figure bent low over me and wrapped me in a pair of strong arms. I breathed deeply. Through the pelting rain I could see my father's face, smell the scent of his cologne, feel the pressure of his hands. "Here you are, sweetie. Oh, honey, I was so worried!"

Overhead, there was a rumble of thunder. Dad clutched me tighter. If it was Dad. I blinked hard, feeling exhausted. *I must have cried myself to sleep here in the tree*, I realized.

"Dad?" I asked, my voice sounding as if it came through a thick fog. *But it can't be Dad*, I thought. *Dad would be the last person on earth to say he was so worried about me.*

"Yes, it's me, Lila," Dad said. His voice caught. "I—I didn't know where you were. When you dashed off—" He swallowed hard. "I thought maybe you'd run away. I just didn't know."

I frowned. Clearly it was Dad—unless I was dreaming again. I sat up a little straighter, realizing it had been a long time since my father had given me a hug. I hadn't felt his arms around me like that for quite a while. *If this is a dream*, I told myself sleepily, *it's an awfully nice one.* I peered at Dad, trying to get his face into focus.

"I was terribly worried," he said again. Raindrops trickled down his forehead, but he didn't even wipe them away. "I'm so glad you're still here."

I wrinkled my nose and wondered how he'd gotten up to where I was. I noticed he was standing on a stepladder. "What time is it?" I asked, my voice still sounding froggy.

Dad shrugged. "Probably two in the morning. I don't know."

Two in the morning? I searched my dad's face. "What about—" I gulped, almost afraid to ask the question. "What about your—you know, your trip to Hong Kong?"

Dad nodded slowly, his hair slick from the rainwater. "I canceled it."

My heart gave a leap. "Really?" I asked, trying not to sound too pleased.

Dad grinned weakly. "That's right," he said. He stroked my shoulder with one hand. "Someone else can take care of the business I had out there. When you—well, when you exploded, I realized that maybe I need to take care of things around here first. Like you, for instance."

I held my breath. This wasn't the father I knew. Now I was sure I would wake up any minute.

Dad was speaking again. "I give you lots of things," he said, "but I guess that's not the same as giving you my time and attention, is it?"

I pinched myself, but I didn't wake up. Maybe this wasn't a dream after all. I didn't trust myself to say anything.

"I think of myself as a generous man," my father went on. "But I realize now that I've been selfish. Selfish in the ways that matter most. Selfish with my time. And selfish with my affection." He stooped lower and stared directly into my eyes. "Will you give me one more chance, Lila?" he asked.

I bit my lip and looked down toward the ground. I didn't know what to say.

Dad squeezed my hand. "I promise you that this will be the start of something new."

The words hit me with such force that I almost fell out of the tree. *The start of something new.* Those were the exact words I'd used the previous Sunday, the night Dad was supposed to take me out to

Chez François. I could see myself sitting in the hair salon, thinking how that dinner would change our relationship. . . .

"The start of something new," Dad repeated, blinking as raindrops streamed into his eyes. But he didn't change his position. "That's a promise, Lila."

Slowly I raised my eyes to meet his. I nodded. "One more chance."

Dad seemed to relax. "Good," he said, and he held me close. "Come on out of the tree and into bed. We'll talk in the morning."

Slowly I walked downstairs Sunday morning, completely clueless about what to expect. Would my dad remember the conversation we'd had the previous night? Would he even be in the house? Deep down I suspected he'd gone to Hong Kong after all.

Assuming I hadn't imagined the whole thing.

I paused on the stairs and sniffed. There was a smell of—muffins. Or something that smelled an awful lot like muffins, only with a few differences that I couldn't exactly place.

Someone was there, all right. And unless it was Mrs. Pervis, back early from her daughter's, there was only one possibility.

I took a deep breath and almost choked. A thick cloud of acrid black smoke was pouring out of the kitchen.

"Dad?" Taking the steps two at a time, I burst

through the kitchen door. "What's going on?"

My father was standing in front of the oven, an apron tied loosely around his Armani suit, waving a spatula in the air to clear the smoke. "I was trying to make muffins," he said dolefully. "As a special surprise for you. But I guess I don't know as much about cooking as I thought."

Quickly I turned off the oven and looked over his shoulder. A muffin tin sat in the center of the rack. Each cup contained something that vaguely resembled muffin batter floating in a sea of cooking oil.

"I don't know what went wrong," Dad said, scratching his head. "I followed the recipe exactly right." He pointed to the cookbook in front of him. "See? Flour, sugar, eggs, everything."

I frowned. My eye scanned the recipe. Not that I knew much about cooking myself, of course, but I'd helped make muffins at the Wakefields' once.

"'Grease the muffin tin,'" I read aloud. I turned to face him. "Dad," I said, "how much oil did you use to grease the tin?"

Dad considered. "Well, I didn't exactly measure," he admitted. "But when I poured a spoonful into each of the cups, it didn't look like enough—so I added some more." He frowned over the top of the spatula. "Did I mess up?"

"You could say that," I agreed, trying not to laugh as I pulled the tin out of the oven and dumped the contents into the sink. "Let's let the disposal take care of them," I said, making a face.

But secretly I was pleased. The muffins would have tasted terrible, that was for sure. Still, it was nice that Dad had taken the time to make them.

And it's the thought that counts, right?

Dad draped an arm around my shoulder. "I have a business appointment with someone today," he said. "With a special client. A *very* special client." He looked at me meaningfully.

My heart sank. I'd hoped he hadn't forgotten the previous night so quickly. Or maybe I'd dreamed it after all. My cheeks reddened, and I kicked an imaginary pebble in front of me. "Oh," I said.

"Whose name is Lila Fowler," Dad added quickly.

"Oh!" My head snapped back up again. "You mean—"

Dad nodded. "We're spending the whole day together," he said. "Just you and me. That's the way you wanted it, isn't it? Well, that's the way I want it too."

I began to grin. "But Dad, I have plans for this afternoon," I said. I didn't, but I wanted to see how he would react. "Me and some of the other Unicorns are going to—"

"Call them and cancel," Dad ordered. He put his hands on his hips, which looked pretty silly considering that he still had the spatula in one hand. "Young lady, you and I are spending some quality time together, whether you like it or not."

"Oh," I said again. Inside I was leaping for joy, but I pulled down the corners of my mouth. "But—"

"No buts, Lila," Dad said. "It's about time I started acting like a real father, and that means discipline. You're not twenty-one yet, you know. Starting today, you're grounded for—let me see— two weeks."

"Two weeks!" I let out a yelp of anguish. "That's ridiculous. All the other girls would only be grounded for—"

For how long? I thought hard. Probably none of the other Unicorns would be grounded for anything like two weeks. On the other hand, none of them would have done such a stupid thing as have a party at their house without asking their dad's permission.

And none of them would have invited half the high school. Without even knowing it.

Maybe my dad was right. I wasn't twenty-one. Maybe, in a lot of ways, I still was a kid. Maybe I wasn't quite ready yet to be on my own and on the loose. Maybe . . .

I turned to face him. "OK," I agreed. "On one condition."

"Condition?" Dad looked bewildered. "What do you mean, on one condition?"

"Just what I said." It felt so good to have my father actually listening to me for a change. "I'll agree to be grounded for two weeks if you agree to be grounded too."

"Me?" Dad touched the edge of the spatula to his apron. "You want to ground me?"

The idea made perfect sense. "That's right," I told him. "It's only fair. If I can be grounded for not following the rules of being a daughter, you can be grounded for forgetting how to be a dad. I'll be grounded—and you promise not to make any business trips for two weeks." I held my breath.

A smile began to crinkle around the corners of Dad's mouth. "You're serious, aren't you?" he said.

I nodded and swallowed hard.

Dad grinned. "All right," he said slowly. "I guess Fowler Enterprises won't go bankrupt if its chief executive officer takes a couple of weeks off to get to know his daughter."

"Good for you, Dad!" The words tumbled out, and I pumped my fist into the air. The world was OK again. My dad really did love me after all. "And I'm—you know. Sorry." It was hard getting the words out, but I felt that it was important. "I— I shouldn't have had the party without asking you." I swallowed hard. "I guess I was in over my head."

Dad winked at me. "Apology accepted. I'm sorry too." He took a deep breath. "So—um—what should we do first?" he asked.

I laughed. My heart felt lighter than it had in a long, long time. "We should make some muffins together for breakfast," I told him. "But there's something else we ought to do first."

"Oh?" Dad cocked his head curiously.

I stepped forward with one foot and extended

my arms toward Dad. "Oh, away down yonder in the state of Arkansas," I sang.

Dad smiled. He reached out toward me. "Where my great-grandpaw met my great-grandmaw," he sang. His eyes twinkled as his big hands grabbed me around the waist, as if the last time we'd done this had just been the day before.

And together we danced all through the house to the strains of "Salty Dog Rag."

Everything is great with Lila . . . but what happens to the Unicorns when Kimberly starts hanging out with their rival club, the Eight Times Eights? Find out in THE UNICORN CLUB #15, **Too Cool for the Unicorns.**

Cool stuff for you and your best friend!

We hope you enjoyed *Twins in Love*. Your opinion is important to us, and we'd love to hear from you. If you are one of the first 100 readers to return this questionnaire, we'll send you this cool stuff (one for you, one for your best friend).

BONNE BELL®
• 2 Stuff Sacks

THE WORLD OF **SweetValley** *Created By FRANCINE PASCAL*
• 2 autographed books

• 2 copies of magazine
Girls'Life

1. Did you like this book? (Check one) ○ I loved it ○ I liked it ○ It was OK
   ○ I didn't like it ○ I hated it
2. Would you recommend this book to a friend? (Check one) ○ Definitely yes
   ○ Probably yes ○ Maybe ○ Probably not ○ Definitely not
3. Is this the first **Sweet Valley Twins** book you've read? ○ Yes
   If not, how many have you read in total? _____
   In the past month? (Check one) ○ 1-2 ○ 3-4 ○ 5+
4. Would you read more **Sweet Valley Twins** books? (Check one)
   ○ Definitely yes ○ Probably yes ○ Maybe ○ Probably not
   ○ Definitely not
5. Have you read any other **Sweet Valley** books? (Check all that apply)
   ○ Sweet Valley Kids ○ The Unicorn Club ○ Sweet Valley High
   ○ Sweet Valley University
   If yes, how many have you read in the past month? _____
6. Did you get this book in the **Sweet Valley Best Friends Twin Pack**? (Check one)
   ○ Yes ○ No
   If yes, where did you first learn about the **Sweet Valley Best Friends Twin Pack**?
   (Check one) ○ Advertisement ○ Store Display ○ Friend
   ○ Other (Please specify)_____
7. Who picked out this book for you? (Check one) ○ I did (reader)
   ○ Parents/Grandparents ○ Friend ○ Other (Please specify)
8. Where was this book bought? ○ Bookstore ○ Grocery Store
   ○ Drugstore ○ Discount Chain Store (like K-Mart)
   ○ Other (Please specify) _____

Your Name_____
Address_____
City_____ State_____ Zip_____
Date of Birth_____/_____/_____

Please send this completed questionnaire to: Sweet Valley Twins, 1540 Broadway, BFYR Marketing, 20th floor, New York, NY 10036